THE CORPSE
NEXT DOOR

The
CORPSE
NEXT
DOOR

JOHN FARRIS

WILDSIDE PRESS

Copyright © 1956 by
Graphic Publishing Company, Inc.
240 West 40 Street
New York, N. Y.

Cover by Oliver Brabbins

1

THE KID was dead. They had cut him down and pulled the twisted shirt from around his neck and two firemen were giving him respiration, but you could tell it was too late.

I turned to the jailer. He stood with thumbs hooked in belt, chewing tobacco, looking at the boy lying on the floor of the cell.

"How long was he hanging there?"

The jailer shrugged. "Ten, fifteen minutes. Goddam, it sure swole his face up, didn't it?"

"Where were you while he was hanging?"

He pushed a knuckle through gray whiskers near his mouth to wipe away tobacco juice. "Downstairs. Where I'm usually at. Wasn't no reason for me to be up here, then. Hell, this is practically a new jail. They ain't supposed to be able to kill themselves in it."

I looked around the cell block. Small steel-and-concrete walls, lights recessed into the ceiling behind glass, bunks bolted to the walls. When a prisoner was locked up he surrendered all items with which he might do harm to himself or others. But Jimmy Herne had knotted part of his shirt carefully around a bar of the bunk and fixed the rest around his neck. He had stretched himself on the floor with his face not quite touching. He had rolled over a couple of times, the shirt tightening into his neck. It takes a while to die that way. He had been patient about it.

I touched one of the firemen on the shoulder. He looked up.

"Any chance?"

"Don't think so, Sergeant. That's a dead face if I ever saw one."

The old jailer leaned against the bars and ruminated. He had a bent shield pinned to one suspender and there were shiny patches on his khaki pants. His lower jaw moved from side to side.

"Well, maybe it saves the state the expense of executing him, but I wisht he didn't have to kick off in my jail."

"Shut up, damn it!"

He looked childishly hurt. "Don't pick on me, I can't help it if I'm old and smell bad. Hell, Sergeant. What you so upset for? He was just another punk. Ain't nobody goin' to miss him."

A doctor hurried down the corridor and into the cell. He bent beside the kid and turned him over on his back. He made his examination quickly but thoroughly.

"Go polish your fire engines, boys. You can't do anything with this one."

"Detective Sergeant Randall," I said absently.

"I can't close his eyes because of protrusion," the doctor explained.

The county stored its bodies at Kenwick's. "We'll call and have a hearse sent around," I said. I looked at the jailer and he took off.

The doctor glanced at the shirt on the cell floor. "That's Jimmy Herne. He took his own life?"

I nodded, my eyes shut. "Yes. He confessed killing Leland Smithell yesterday. We should have had somebody watching him."

The doctor's heavy dark eyes were troubled. "I visited Smithell's house a couple of times since Jimmy went to work for him. I'm sure he treated the boy well. Why would he kill the man who befriended him? Sometimes I don't understand things."

"You should have been a cop, doctor. Thanks for coming over."

The old jailer wandered in and spread a blanket over Jimmy Herne. Watching this, I had the feeling in the back of my mind, the chill knowledge of trouble ahead, and I breathed heavily.

"Doc," the jailer said, "I've got an elbow been giving me

trouble since I fell on it a couple of weeks back and I've been wondering if you couldn't . . ."

The doctor picked up his bag.

"Aw, hell," the jailer grumbled, and went away to call the cemetery wagon.

As the doctor walked out, the firemen were packing up their respirator. They nodded to me and left. I was alone with Jimmy Herne and I didn't like it. I could feel his eyes, still open and staring under the blanket. I could hear him wailing, "I didn't do it, I didn't do it, I didn't . . ."

Phil Naar waited in the corridor outside the cell, leaning against the bars, wetting the tip of an unlit cigarette. He wore an old gray suit that looked like he had been born in it and his hat was pushed back on his head so that white hair fell over his forehead from beneath the brim. His face is old. He's spent nineteen years being a cop and he looks like one. I've been a cop for nine years and I look like a hood.

"Not nice, hey?" Phil said. "He wasn't a bad kid. I sort of felt sorry for the little monkey. I knew he was weak, but I felt sorry for him. Guts show up in the strangest places, don't they?"

Rolling over, once, twice, the shirt tightening . . .

"Let's get the hell out," I said.

We walked through the door of the cell block and out to the landing, where we picked up our guns. A guard pushed a lever that shut the main door. On his switchboard he has levers that can open each cell individually, or all at once. It's really a nice jail, if you like jails.

One of the regulars, wearing denims wet at the knees, was scrubbing the metal stairs with an old brush and a pot of water foaming with disinfectant. The man held the bottle in one hand and looked at the amber liquid thoughtfully.

"No, no, Dudley," I said. "It'll put pine knots on your stomach."

He looked guiltily at us and picked up the brush.

We walked on down the steps.

Phil squinted at hard sunlight that came through a skylight at the top of the stairwell. "Are you the one going to tell her?"

I hesitated, thinking about it. "I suppose so. I don't want

to. I'll have to tell Gulliver first. He'll feel left out if I don't."

We split up in the hall downstairs, Phil continuing on to circuit court. I went outside and down the street to the Cheyney police department.

SAM GULLIVER WAS IN HIS OFFICE WITH THE DOOR OPEN SO I went on in. He was reading a letter from the National Association of Police Chiefs. I waited until he was through.

"What was the excitement at the jail?" he said, putting the letter aside.

"Jimmy Herne," I said. "He hanged himself. With his shirt."

That's the thing about Gulliver. I expected him to be a little surprised at least, for God's sake. But he just sat there and lit a cigar and all he said was, "Did he?"

I nodded.

"Dead, I guess."

"Sure."

He drew on the cigar. "Well, so much for that one. I didn't think he had enough backbone for a stunt like that."

"Doesn't it make any difference to you?"

He was a little surprised. "No. He was as good as dead anyway. He just saved a lot of trouble. You send the stiff to Kenwick's?"

"Sure." I was getting a little irritated. He was acting like a scoutmaster again.

He looked at his cigar and he looked out the window. He looked at me. "Well, I guess that's all. Anything else, Bill?"

"I guess not. What happens if Kenwick finds bruises when he strips the kid? You know Kenwick talks like a four-party line."

Gulliver waved the cigar. "Rumors. They don't mean anything." He slid his roller chair a little closer to the desk. "You know better, Bill. I work better than that. I never bruise anybody. There are other ways."

I knew. There are several ways to jar a man loose from his senses. Gulliver has big hands. The heels of his palms are thick. He uses them against the temples of a suspect and never works up a sweat.

Gulliver smiled a little and picked up a letter. "Look here, Bill."

I took the letter offered and glanced at it. It was from the mayor, commending Chief Gulliver on his expeditious work in capturing Jimmy Herne and obtaining a confession of the murder of Smithell, "one of our outstanding local citizens." I figured the mayor's secretary was on vacation and nobody was around to read the papers to him. The Highway Patrol, not Cheyney police, had captured Jimmy in the railroad yards of a small town seventy miles north of Cheyney.

I read as much as I could stand and surrendered the letter. Gulliver was pleased so I had to get out the needle.

"You're proud of this one, aren't you?"

Maybe I sounded sullen. Gulliver frowned.

"Sure I am." He looked at his stiff left wrist, which lay on the desk top, the two frozen fingers of his hand curled. A souvenir of his days as a rookie cop in St. Louis, which had finished him with the St. Louis police. Every now and then, when he feels a compulsion to hate something, he looks at the wrist. He hates himself for it, for because of it he is not whole and strong as he thinks he needs to be. But most of all he hates those who did it to him, the two kids who must have been like Jimmy Herne, but more vicious.

"I admit there wasn't much to it, just a matter of pounding away until the kid came around. The evidence was conclusive, fingerprints all over the jewelry box, Smithell's wallet empty. Jimmy's past record, and the fact that he ran away."

He looked up sharply, as if wondering why the hell he was explaining.

"I guess you'd better notify the Francis girl," he said. "Tell her Jimmy's dead."

"Okay."

Gulliver put a thumb against his teeth. He was thinking about something. "I thought I was going to have to coax you. You generally gripe like hell when you have to visit bereaved relatives." A little smile touched his face. "I guess it's that girl. You seem to have gotten to know her pretty well in the last four days." He stretched and the chair creaked.

He put one arm over the back of the chair, so his upper arm flattened out.

Gulliver has arms broad as horse's thighs. I've seen tough cons get sweaty just looking at him.

"You even helped her find a lawyer," he said, a smooth empty expression on his face.

I could feel it coming then, like you can feel the pressure of a hard storm behind piled dark clouds.

"I just suggested someone she might get to help Jimmy. She didn't have much money. I didn't want her to waste it on somebody who wouldn't be any good for the kid." I wished I hadn't spoken. I didn't have to explain anything to him.

He brought the cigar out of an ash-tray and traced his lower lip with the wet end of it. Unexpectedly, he smiled. He has a smile like a baby when he wants to use it.

"Oh, I didn't mean anything, Bill. It's okay with me." His eyes said he was remembering. "That Stella Francis . . . now there's a nice little piece. Yes, yes."

"She isn't a piece, Gulliver."

He clamped down on the end of the cigar. There was no more smoothness in his face. "I think she is. I think she's a cheap little piece. I think she's a cheap little lay like every other twist from that side of the river and don't you by God call me Gulliver again without putting Chief in front of it!"

"Yes—*sir*."

He was silent for a while, looking at me without anger, almost morosely. If you know something of Gulliver, you know his moods, as shifting and unexpected and treacherous as the sand bars that come and go in the big river.

He picked up a pencil, pinched the eraser and rubbed at a spot on one fingernail, waiting for me to tell him I was ready to be good.

When I didn't, he said, "I want you to make a tour of Foundry Road about twelve-thirty or one tonight. Investigate every parked car, get names and addresses. Three or four dozen. We've been getting complaints from parents about all the kids necking out there. Throw a scare into 'em."

I put my teeth together, cutting off an angry protest. What a crock. "All right."

"Get out of here now, Bill," he said wearily. "Go tell the Francis girl her cousin killed himself because he had a guilty conscience." He looked at me bleakly for a second longer, then took the letter from the mayor and stroked it with his good hand and started reading it again, but he didn't seem to be getting any pleasure from the words.

THE RIDGE IS A SPINE OF LAND NORTH OF THE BIG RIVER, usually above high-water level, and stretching across the rich lowlands almost to the rise of bluffs and shaggy domes of hills. This is an area of decay, largely abandoned by the old settlers who depended on river trade for their living when the unpredictable river made a new bed farther south. The Ridge was left to the lap of flood water, to fade and grow bleak in the sun. I knew the people who lived there and worked in the mills and small factories. I knew the kids like Jimmy Herne, who were unable to resist the relentless pressure of despair.

I parked in front of the crippled old rooming-house on Davis Street and went upstairs to Stella Francis' room.

Her door stood open. She was inside, near the windows, ironing a dress. The sun was low in the west now, but the old house had soaked up heat all day and the small breeze pushing at the net curtains had little effect on the laden air.

Stella was wearing only a slip, wet under the arms, and the edges of her dusty blonde hair were damp against her forehead. There was a radio on in the room, turned low.

She glanced over one shoulder. "Bill? Come in. Be through with this in a minute."

On a small table with the radio stood a pitcher of ice water. I ducked under a wire stretched across the small room from which Stella's clothes hung and lifted the pitcher. The radio was now saying, "And just half an hour ago this afternoon, at the county jail . . ." and I spilled some of the water in my haste to find another station.

I reached over Stella's shoulder with the misty pitcher. She upended the iron and took the pitcher in both hands, child-fashion, drank, then brushed the hair back from her forehead. Her hair is coarse, but not stiff and dry, cut at the base of her neck, the edges uneven and curled up slightly. In front the blonde hair is like a great mane that can either sweep over her forehead or be brushed back in a wave.

She put down the water pitcher with a sound of appreciation and looked up at me, her green eyes bright and clear, smiling. She seemed so young that it was strange to remember what the rest of her was like, beneath the slip.

I touched her wet shoulder lightly and took a bath towel from a nearby chair. "A bit damp, lady." I toweled off the perspiration, then dabbed at her forehead. I kissed her on the tip of her nose.

Her mouth opened slightly and I kissed her again, seeing the look of sleepy pleasure in those green eyes, the subtle touch of woman-wisdom, at odds with her youthful appearance. Her skin is surprisingly youthful and good though not unmarked. It seemed, as I kissed her, that I had known her for so long—much longer than four days—known the quick one-sided smile, the somber shadows of knowledge that crept into her eyes at times, the fine firm body. I felt that I had never really known myself until I had met her.

"Very good," she said, pleased, when we parted. She made a face at the ironing board. "I hate to iron. Sit down and take a load off those cop's feet, Bill. Excuse the slip. It's so hot in this room."

"There are other places to live," I reminded her.

"But not as cheap." She walked barefoot to the bed and sat and looked at me curiously. "What brings you across the river, Bill? Something about Jimmy?"

I hesitated. She was instantly aware of my uncertainty, and a protective wariness narrowed her eyes.

"About Jimmy," I said. I knew my face must be coloring. "Stella," I said, not looking at her, "the boy was in a bad way. A couple of previous arrests and the murder confession. It didn't look good for him."

I knew I was blundering off in the wrong direction but I couldn't help it.

Her voice became strident in a way that I disliked. "Jimmy's lawyer said that maybe they couldn't prove premeditation. Did he change his mind? Bill . . . " There was a thin sound of fear.

"That's not what I mean," I said desperately. "Jimmy . . . I guess he . . . got tired, or scared or something. Of waiting, and not knowing." Her head came up and she looked at me incredulously. "I don't know why," I said. My mouth was very dry. "He hanged himself this afternoon. With his shirt. I don't know why. But he's dead. I'm sorry, Stella."

She stopped breathing for a moment and her fingers loosened in her lap. She was still looking at me with the same uncomprehending expression. She put her hands between her knees and pressed her legs together hard, so that the calves touched, and her head inclined forward, the mane of blonde hair dangling over her forehead. Her breasts moved erratically as she breathed.

"Stella . . ." I said helplessly.

She began to cry, with gulping irregular sobs. She slid off the bed, kneeled on the floor, holding her head like a sick dog, and cried.

I sat beside her on the floor and held her, her face soft against my neck. She smelled of sweat and shampoo and woman-odor.

I leaned back against the bed and held her and felt her tears warm on my cheek, knowing the tragedy of shattered hopes more tragic because the hopes were founded in futility, and it had always been that way for her, because she was a Ridge girl. And that was not all I knew. I knew she was poor and nearly alone when she quit high school her first year because she was tired of wearing the same dress three times a week and washing out the same underwear every night. I knew there was a boy, somewhere in her life, shot dead by the owner of a liquor store during an attempted holdup. I knew she worked nights as a waitress and saved her money patiently for the day when she could leave the Ridge and I knew there was a streak of honesty and independence in her a mile wide.

I knew, most of all, that I had wanted her from the first moment I had seen her, in the hall of the police station, when she had spit in Gulliver's face because he wouldn't let her see her cousin.

Holding the good comfortable weight of her against me as she cried I remembered last night, on the edge of the deep silent river. I had taken her there, to my river, where I liked to go and sit on a beached log beside the eddying water and look to the bluffs on the other side and think. The river-washed sand had been fine and smooth. It had been warm and quiet and very dark and there had been a strange terror about being close to the great moving river, so that it seemed almost inevitable we would lie close and eagerly, bonded by the searing kisses. I knew, as a man will know, that she wanted more, much more . . .

She's not a piece, Gulliver.

Yet she had been prepared for me. She had been prepared to receive me, prepared in a way nice young girls usually are not.

I understood that on the Ridge life is hard and uncertain and there is an attitude of get it while you can. Lust is solid beneath the surface of restless lives and chastity doesn't exist where there is no reason for it to.

Yes, I knew Stella, yet I didn't know her. I didn't know why it had been that way on the bank of the river. Now she squirmed and sobbed in my arms.

"Bill . . . Bill, the poor little guy . . ."

"There's nothing you can do."

She turned away from me and rubbed at her reddened eyes. "He was such a little kid," she said. The violence of her grief had given her hiccups. "Such a little . . . underweight kid. He never had a break, Bill. Never . . . had one goddam tiny break in his whole . . . goddam life."

She stood up awkwardly and sniffed and rubbed the back of her hand against her eyes and walked out of the bedroom, down the hall to the bath.

I went to the window and looked out, at the acre or so of dumped trash where the city was trying to create a fill, at the patchwork fields beyond and the fringe of trees bounding the river.

I felt as though I had no business being there, in her room, with the hard gun at my side and the badge in my pocket. A Ridge boy had died, and I was intruding on the wrenching grief of someone who had cared for him, who had recognized his consuming need for being wanted and protected. Well, I was a cop. I had put on the badge and I was right. Those, like Jimmy Herne, who made my work, were wrong. It was the only way I could think, the way all of us had to think. When you started making excuses for them, wondering why, your effectiveness as a cop goes. That's what Gulliver had told me, and probably it was the truth. *Never give them a break, Bill. When you start giving them a break, they'll kill you. One way or another.* That's what Gulliver had said, many times.

Yet I had tried to help Jimmy Herne, in a small way; not because I was sorry for him, but because of Stella.

I had to think about her, and the four days, about her instinctive dislike for me because of the badge, the dislike that had disappeared, until the fulfillment for both of us, last night. I had to wonder if it had been for both of us . . .

Stella returned. Her eyes had dried and there was a tight expression on her face. I tried to think of something to say, some small words of comfort. I couldn't.

She sat on the bed again, her legs spread beneath the slip, her shoulders rounded. "He hated prison," she said, as if remembering every thing about him was important. "He nearly went crazy those eight months in the reformatory. He said he'd never go back. Never. He used to talk when he was staying with me. He'd sit and talk about what he was going to do. He wasn't full of crap any more about being a big man, about the jobs he would pull. He was almost humble, wanting to find a good job and stick with it, become useful. He used to get that scared look every time he thought about the reformatory. Not just ordinary scared. When Mr. Smithell heard about him from the parole board, I thought that—well, that it would be okay."

She got up and went to the dresser and picked up her comb. She pulled it through the thick mane of hair, combing it down over her eyes.

"Maybe what happened was best," I said. "His lawyer

was working for him, Stella. But he couldn't have done much better for Jimmy than a life term."

She whipped the comb from her hair and flung it at me. I was startled by the cold fury in her eyes. She stood spraddle-legged with her breasts outthrust, fists hard near her thighs.

"No!" she yelled. "It wasn't for the best because Jimmy didn't do it! He wasn't any more guilty than I am and he'd be free right now instead of dead if it wasn't for that dirty Gulliver!"

I took her by the shoulders. "Stella, Jimmy confessed. He confessed because he was guilty and he knew it and you know it."

"Confession," she said, as if she were going to spit. Her voice trembled. "I know all about confessions like that. The last time I visited Jimmy he could hardly move or talk to me. He kept getting his words mixed up. You think I'm simple? I know what goes on in the basement uptown. I've seen others who came out of there. Jimmy confessed because he didn't have any choice. Gulliver beat him to a pulp."

"Shut up," I said, my teeth together. "Shut up, unless you can prove it!" I could feel the deep pressure of unreasoning anger rising against her and I knew I was hurting her as she twisted under my hands.

"Why don't you tell me it's not true?"

I glared at her.

"Because you can't," she almost yelled. "Because Gulliver did beat him. Jimmy was just a kid who couldn't fight back. Gulliver needed a sucker and he picked on Jimmy and now Jimmy's dead!"

I released her, turned up the radio, then kicked the door shut, trying to control my rage. "Jimmy cleaned out Smith-ell's jewelry box, stripped his wallet and took his watch," I said monotonously. "Then he ran for it. That doesn't sound very innocent to me."

"You know why he ran," she cried, fresh tears in her eyes. "He came home from the picture show and Smithell was dead on the floor and he knew you lousy cops would try to pin it on him."

I stood very close to her. "Now you said it. Why don't

you finish? I'm one of those lousy cops. I suppose you think
I hit the kid too. I suppose you think I beat on him when
Gulliver was tired. Is that what you think?"

"Maybe you did! If he was so guilty you didn't have to
beat him to find out!" she sobbed. She stepped back and hit
me hard in the face with her open palm. It really rocked me.
Her eyes brimmed. She hit me again, almost swinging from
the heels, then staggered to the bed, fell across it.

"Ah, Bill," she said. "Ah, Bill, he was such a sweet little
kid. If you knew him like I did . . ."

I rubbed my face gently where she had hit me. I went to
her and sat beside her and put my arm across her shoulders.

After a while she sat up on the bed, put her arms around
her knees. She looked at me uncertainly. "Are you angry?"

"Little idiot," I said.

"I was so hurt," she said. "It's always been like that, when
I'm hurt."

"I know. You had to hit something."

"Bill, you wouldn't lie to me."

"About what?"

"Did Gulliver hit him?"

"Is it important now?"

"Yes," she said, "it is. I know Jimmy's dead, and nothing
can change that. But I want to know why he died."

I seized one of her hands and held it. "You've got to
remember how it must have been with him, Stella. You believed in him. He knew how disappointed you were. Maybe
he couldn't take that."

"Yes, I guess so," she said remotely. I wondered how much
Jimmy had talked to her. A silence gathered between us, a
silence I didn't like. Then she said softly, "Did he? Gulliver?"

"For Christ's sake," I said. Then I said, "Yes, I suppose he
did. Gulliver is a tough violent man, Stella. He's been a cop
all his life. Sometimes he gets fed up with all the dirty people.
Sometimes he loses his temper and hits a man in custody."

"Were you with him when he was questioning Jimmy?"

"Yes."

"Did you see him hit Jimmy?"

I didn't like the calm way she was speaking, and I didn't

like being forced into a lie, into an expression of loyalty for Gulliver I didn't feel.

"No," I said, thinking of the movement of Gulliver's stocky body, the hands going out, the hard splatting sounds as his palms rocked Jimmy's head.

Come on, Jimmy, I got enough right now to turn you over to the county attorney, but I want to make good and sure. Tell me you killed him.

No. No. No. No. No.

Where did you get that thirty bucks, Jimmy?

He gave it to me—to buy a suit.

I guess you wanted more. I guess that's it, isn't it Jimmy?

"No," I said. "I didn't see him hit Jimmy."

She propped herself on one elbow and looked at me. "Bill," she said earnestly, "do you honestly believe Jimmy was guilty?"

I looked at her for a long time. "Yes," I said quietly. "Yes, Stella. I think Jimmy killed him."

Her eyes closed and she settled back against the pillow. "Bill," she said, "I'd like to be alone now."

I touched her leg but she didn't respond. I got off the bed and lit a cigarette. She didn't move or look at me.

"When will I see you again?"

"I don't know, Bill," she said, as if it didn't matter at all, had never mattered. "I don't know."

I left her then, beginning to feel a restless anger I couldn't define.

2

THAT night I was having a drink in the bar of Roxy Marko's place on Highway 44 when Miller Starkey came over.

"Evening, Sergeant," he said amiably, sliding onto a stool next to mine.

I wasn't particularly interested in talking to him, or to anyone else, but I returned his greeting.

"Whiskey sour, Max," he advised the bartender. "Buy you a drink, Sergeant?"

"This'll hold me for a while, Mr. Starkey. How are the girls?"

"Fine. Fine." He beamed at me. He was proud of his two girls. "Pootsie—that's Alice, you know—is expecting again. And Juanita is president of her sorority up at State."

I nodded. The Starkey girls were famous in Cheyney. Born a year apart, they had raised hell from the cradle on, growing boisterous and beautiful. The last time I had seen them together they were under arrest on a shoplifting charge. Gulliver and Starkey had held a fast conference and the girls weren't booked. Charges were subsequently dropped.

In return for this favor, Starkey allowed police personnel to buy everything in his men's shop, the best in town, for twenty-five percent off. It meant, to me and to most of the others, the difference between feeling almost dressed and well dressed on the same salary.

Miller Starkey was unimpressively built, very near-sighted, with gray hair that stuck straight up from his scalp about four inches. It was hard to imagine how he could have been responsible for the Starkey women.

Max delivered the whiskey sour and Starkey fondled the

glass before drinking, smiling. He smiles all the time. I suppose it's a mannerism. Like nose-picking.

"So Jimmy Herne committed suicide," he said. "I guess that wraps up the case, doesn't it, Sergeant?"

"As far as we're concerned it was already wrapped up."

He lost some of his man-to-man chumminess. "Certainly. I only meant—" He poked in embarrassment at his glass.

The small bar was cool and uncrowded. To my left were glass panels partially covered with soft blue drapes and on the other side of the glass was the dining room, almost filled to capacity despite the fact that it was past nine o'clock.

"You know, I . . . I wanted to talk to you about Mr. Smithell," Starkey said.

"How's that, Mr. Starkey?"

The smile again. "It's this way. Mr. Smithell owed rather a large bill at the time of—his death—and I don't quite know . . ."

"Oh. I wouldn't worry about that, Mr. Starkey. See Nordin Kaylor and I'm sure he'll take care of it." Nordin Kaylor had been Smithell's partner in two Cheyney automobile agencies.

"Certainly. I should have thought of that." The unreal whiteness of his false teeth touched the rim of the glass. "I knew Mr. Smithell had only lived in Cheyney about three years and had no relatives here, so you understand . . ."

I looked toward the dining room just as Roxy Marko was passing. He noticed me and waved, so I lifted my glass in his direction.

"It seems as if there's no gratitude in the world," Starkey said. "Here Mr. Smithell was willing to take on a boy who had been in the reformatory, let him live in his house, pay him a good salary. Probably the boy was planning all along to rob him when the opportunity arose. Did you ever learn the full story, Sergeant? The papers were so vague . . ."

He looked at me avidly over his glass, perhaps anticipating a party that week, a group of his friends discussing the same subject, himself saying casually, "Now, Sergeant Randall told me . . ."

"His confession was very complete," I said. I didn't say

that Gulliver had written it and Jimmy had contributed only his signature.

You returned to the house about eleven, after the picture show. And he was asleep. You figured it was as good a time as any. But you didn't figure he'd wake up. You had to hit him. You didn't mean to hit him so hard. Then you took the watch and money along with the jewelry. Three thousand bucks worth. You didn't know he was dead when you packed your stuff and beat it, did you? Later when you found out how hot you were you got rid of the jewelry and watch, dumped them in the river somewhere. That's how it was, huh, Jimmy? Just sign here, boy, and we'll leave you alone.

"The very day . . . " Starkey said.

"Excuse me," I said. "I'm afraid my mind was wondering."

His smile looked like it had been stepped on. "I just said that the very day Jimmy killed him, Mr. Smithell was planning to buy Jimmy a new suit."

I felt vaguely apprehensive. "Did you read that in the paper, Mr. Starkey?"

"Why—no. Mr. Smithell called me that afternoon, before he was murdered, told me Jimmy was coming in next day for a fitting. He wanted me to sort of influence the boy's choice so Jimmy wouldn't come home with anything drastic in color or style."

I took a longer swallow of my drink than usual and never tasted it. "I see. Was he going to charge it?"

"No. He told me that he'd given the money to Jimmy. Thirty dollars. He didn't want the boy picking out something too expensive, so he thought it might make Jimmy feel more responsible if he paid for it himself."

Starkey looked past me with an expression of mock surprise. "Well, here comes my wife. I thought maybe she'd fallen in." He chuckled. "Thanks for the advice, Sergeant. Drop by the store some time this week. We've received a shipment of those pastel shirts you like so much."

"Thanks, Mr. Starkey." I sat there after he had left, feeling a slow gathering sickness in my stomach, a sickness that couldn't be vomited up. I gulped the rest of the drink and looked at myself in the mirror behind the bar. I was ugly this night.

Someone tapped my shoulder. "Excuse me."

I turned and looked at a waiter.

"Mr. Marko sent me, Sergeant Randall. He'd like for you to have a drink with him in his office."

I wanted to say no, say that I had to go somewhere, away from the pressure I was feeling, like lazy tightening coils. But there was no way I could refuse.

I left the bar and crossed the foyer, went up a flight of stairs to Roxy's office. I knocked and was invited in.

As soon as I opened the door I saw Gulliver inside.

He was sitting in one of Roxy's big white leather chairs with his shoes off and a drink in his hand. He smiled peacefully at me.

"Hello, Chief. Roxy," I said, nodding. Roxy was fixing himself a drink at his desk. He looked at me inquisitively.

"Bill?"

"Bourbon over ice, a little sparkling."

"A man of simple tastes," Gulliver said. I could tell he was in a mellow mood. He lifted his glass at me and winked. "Ten years old. Roxy's putting on the dog tonight."

Roxy smiled slightly. He's a small man, about five feet five, with a gentle expression that never seems to change. He has gleaming copper-colored hair and a small mustache, and there are clusters of freckles around his eyes, growing darker with age.

He handed me my drink and waved me to a chair. Roxy enjoys luxury. The office walls are padded halfway to the ceiling with the same white leather as the chairs carry, and on one corner stretches a curved sofa that is part of the wall.

On one wall hangs a large oil painting of a nude man and woman. It's Gulliver's favorite picture. I've seen him sit in that chair and look at the picture for half an hour, pouring drinks into his belly, and at the end of that time a little smile will start and he'll laugh his head off and then he won't look at the picture for a while. I've never seen Roxy look at it.

"How did the Francis girl take it this afternoon?" Gulliver said.

I looked at him. His eyes were guileless.

"Pretty hard," I said. "They were close, as people are in that part of town. She was hoping, all the time, that something could be done. She didn't really believe it, but she was hoping."

"She's a fighter," Gulliver said sympathetically. "Lot of backbone. Not like Jimmy." He shook his head and sighed. "I always hate to see a good fighter beaten."

Roxy drank silently behind his desk, watching us almost shyly. He takes his whiskey in a shot glass along with a larger glass of ice and soda, drinking some of the soda, then throwing a little whiskey on top of it.

Gulliver stretched happily, one hand on his belly, the belly with the deceptive slab of fat and the corded muscles underneath. He looked at the picture and his lips were full and heavy at the corners, his eyes a little restive. He drank slowly. Gulliver has a liquor stomach, lined with sponges. He can throw down better than a pint of whiskey and he won't look drunk, if you don't know what to look for. Then he'll put the bottle down and fold his hands over his stomach and sleep for twenty-four hours, unless somebody sets him on fire. But he wasn't drinking that fast tonight and I knew, the different sort of way he was looking at the picture, that tonight maybe it would be Alise, the big red-headed one who liked to go down fighting. Roxy was a good friend. He was big, maybe the biggest, in local politics. He owned six gin mills besides this place, the big tourist court and restaurant, and other odds and ends, like Alise. In an hour, maybe, Gulliver would feel the whiskey he was drinking so slowly now, feel it just right, and he would look at Roxy and Roxy would pick up the phone. Not that it was that kind of tourist court. It was just that Roxy was such a good friend.

And I had a feeling, looking at Gulliver, that I wanted to destroy the mood he was constructing, that I was going to anyway, because the good whiskey hadn't rinsed the dead metal taste of fear from my mouth.

"You know, Bill," Gulliver said, "I shouldn't have said what I did this afternoon. About the Francis girl. I don't blame you for maybe getting a little peeved. Forget what I said about Foundry Road. I'll have one of the patrol cars drive by. Not much use in it, anyway. Kids are going to get their snatch, one way or another."

He gave me that smile, so I would feel all warm and good and gee-Chief-you-mean-I'm-part-of-the-team-again?

"Thanks," I said.

Gulliver got up and walked over to Roxy's desk, helped himself to the whiskey. "Say, Bill, when was it that soldier came in?"

"The one who beefed about dropping three hundred bucks in that poker game at the Regal? Monday night, I think."

"Yeah." Gulliver looked at Roxy. "We've had some kick-backs lately, Roxy. Nothing serious. A couple of soldiers who dropped their rolls and wanted to start something. But if somebody from Fort McHale gets took in one of your games and goes to his C.O. I'm liable to hear from the Provost."

"Some people are just unlucky at poker, Sam," Roxy said. "You know that. If everybody won I'd be out of business."

I couldn't see his eyes where I was sitting, but I knew they were as bright and cold as morning sunlight on pond ice, despite his soft, almost whispering voice. A lot of people who thought they knew Roxy had never looked directly into those eyes. You could interpret Roxy a lot of different ways. I had my own ideas about him. So did Gulliver. He handled Roxy carefully. He had heard the story, too.

"Sure, I know," Gulliver said. "It was just the usual sour grapes routine. But trouble could start. Maybe you ought to get in touch with your steerer down at the Fort. Bring him up here for a little talk. Make sure he's more careful who he sends this way. Then if somebody drops a wad he won't kick because he has sense enough to know it wasn't his night."

Roxy nodded. "I guess I'd better. Thanks for telling me, Sam."

I had no taste for that kind of talk. It was part of the discontent I had felt for a long time, the arrangements Gulliver had, with Miller Starkey, with Roxy. I suppose there was nothing wrong with us taking advantage of Starkey's discount. It was no secret in town. And there was nothing wrong with Roxy's poker games in the hotel, although not so many people knew about that. Or the women outside the bus station and servicemen's center, who dressed well and were discreet about it and you would never guess what they were. They paid by the month, to Gulliver, and had helped finance a new squad car. There was nothing really wrong, you could argue, because no money went into private pockets. But I felt the discontent, because the Starkey girls liked to drive fast, and some day there might be a wreck, and Starkey would remind Gulliver of the discount. And I remembered the look in Roxy's eyes, as if he were seeing something a long way off, a bigger and better Roxy, and I remembered the story. I wondered if anybody could really handle Roxy, as Gulliver said he could.

"I had a talk with Miller Starkey downstairs," I said.

Gulliver dropped clear cylinders of fresh ice into his new drink. "How's the old man getting along?"

"All right, I guess. He wanted to talk about Jimmy Herne."

"He would," Gulliver said, tasting his drink, then adding a touch of sparkling.

"He said that Smithell called him the afternoon before he was murdered. Smithell told Starkey he was sending Jimmy Herne in next day to buy a suit. Jimmy had the money. He was going to learn responsibility by paying for it himself."

Gulliver was about to say something, but didn't. The mood had been as light and slender as fine blonde hair and I had snapped it. He was concentrating on recalling it but I knew he wouldn't.

"He had thirty bucks to buy the suit with," I said.

Gulliver went back to his chair. Roxy watched both of us as if he were peeking through a keyhole.

"Ah, let's forget about Smithell and the kid, for God's sake," Gulliver said. "I put in a hard week's work on that one. It's finished. I don't want to talk about it."

"Jimmy had exactly thirty bucks in his pocket when he was picked up," I said stubbornly, trying to make him see it.

It's a funny thing about Gulliver. When he's starting to burn, he tries to flex that stiff left wrist. The harder he tries, the madder he gets, because it only moves a quarter-inch in any direction. He was trying to flex it now, looking at it with shiny intent eyes.

"Now, listen, Bill. I don't know why you keep talking after I told you to shut—to keep still. Roxy's our host and I don"t want to bother him with police business. I'm telling you to forget it."

Maybe I wouldn't have kept on then, but he picked exactly the wrong tone to use, bawling me out like I was a kid. "Jimmy said he got the thirty bucks to buy a suit. It looks like he was telling the truth. Maybe he was telling the truth about the other things. Maybe he didn't kill Smithell." I threw in the last without even thinking, because I was getting sore.

Gulliver gave me a furious look. He stood up, leaving his drink on the floor. "All right, if you're not going to shut up I'll get out of here. I don't know what gets into you, Bill. I just want a quiet little evening and you go and spoil the whole goddam thing. I don't know what's the matter with you, Bill."

Roxy said, "Sam, do you want me to call—"

"No!" Gulliver raged. "I'm too upset for any pigeon plucking tonight. I'm just going to get the hell out of here."

He started for the door and was halfway across the rug when he remembered he had left his shoes in front of the chair. He hesitated, then turned around and went back for them. He carried the shoes in one hand and made for the door and I felt a laugh coming. I suppressed it because there is nothing funny about Gulliver when he's angry.

The door closed behind him and there was a loaded silence that slowly became weary.

I drank from my glass, feeling sort of ridiculous and a little bit sorry. "Well, I've got to open my goddam mouth," I said. "I'm sorry, Roxy."

"You ought to be," Roxy said, but his voice, as usual, was mild. "I suppose it's none of my business, but you ought to forget about it, Bill. Or take it up with him later. You picked a bad time."

"I know."

Roxy went through his ritual of putting a little whiskey down. "We were talking about you, Bill, before you came up. Gulliver likes you, Bill. He really likes you. And respects you, too. He knows you've got the guts to stand up to him. But you shouldn't overdo it. I don't know much about the case you and Sam have been working on. I know he was satisfied that the case was closed. You seem intent on reopening it."

"Look, Roxy," I said, "I'm a cop. I'm supposed to keep an open mind about the cases I investigate. Jimmy Herne confessed he killed Smithell. I don't think he would have said one word about killing the old man if he hadn't done it, because he had everything to lose. Gulliver worked on him, though. Nothing unusual. But he worked on him. I don't know how much the kid could take. I don't know if he could have been made under duress to confess a murder he didn't commit. I thought the kid was guilty. I still think so. I learned tonight that one of the statements Jimmy made, about where he got the money, stands up. That's all. I was just telling Gulliver. Maybe I said more than necessary. He shouldn't have told me to keep my mouth shut in front of you."

"Let's forget it, Bill. Sam will cool off. I was saying, Bill, that he likes you. We were talking about Endicott earlier."

Endicott had been assistant chief of police until his death two month ago. "Yeah?"

"Gulliver thinks you could fill that job and retain your present duties—for forty dollars a month more."

"It would be nice," I said, surprised.

Roxy smiled. "You've got a good future in Cheyney, Bill. I thought you'd like to know. That's why I'm cautioning you not to assert yourself so much with Gulliver. Not that you should let yourself be pushed around. You know."

"I think so."

"If you're staying for dinner," Roxy said, "I'll call down to Rudy and have him put your steak on."

While he was on the phone, I went to his desk and mixed myself another drink, not thinking about Gulliver now, but about Roxy, who thought I had a good future in Cheyney. Roxy with the eyes of cold purpose. I was lucky to be so popular with everybody.

LATER, WHEN I WAS LEAVING, I WALKED OVER TO THE SHED-like bungalow that housed some of Roxy's kitchen help and a couple of chambermaids who cleaned up in the motel. One of them had been involved in some petty thefts on the grounds a couple of months before, but I had let her off after she had restored the pilfered property to the transient guest, who didn't want to be delayed by pressing charges.

I got her to step outside with me. She was a gray, wispy woman on the other side of fifty. "Been behaving yourself, Barbara?"

"Oh, sure, Sergeant. Sure I have. I'll never do anything like that again."

"Look, Barbara. You have a set of master keys, don't you? I mean, you have to get into all the cabins and rooms and places."

"Sure. I have a set and so does the other girl."

"Does she clean Roxy's office, or do you?"

"I do. But—"

"I just want the key for an hour or so. I'll get it right back to you. Nobody will know."

"Oh, I couldn't do that, Sergeant!"

"You want me to mention about that stealing? You want me to tell Roxy, or maybe Chief Gulliver?"

She said nothing more. I drove the key over to a hardware retailer in Rocky Spring, a friend of mine. Rocky Spring lies about twenty miles south on the highway, and by the time I got there my friend had gone to bed. I woke him, got him to go to his store. There he duplicated the key for me, and I drove back to Cheyney, returning the original to old Barbara.

THERE IS AN OLD BLACKTOP ROAD SOUTH OF ROXY'S PLACE that is a quick way into town. It winds for four miles through farmland and is called Foundry Road because of an old ironworks built along it somewhere. The kids like the road because it's always dark and rarely used and there are many dirt side roads.

Heat lightning glimmered in the thick clouds over the river valley to the north and there was a musty wet smell of rain in the air as I drove along the road, away from Roxy's. As I took a curve my headlights revealed a truck pulled almost off the road. A man stood beside the truck. I slowed as I saw the car in the ditch on the other side.

I pulled across the road and parked facing the truck. It was carrying a load of furniture with a tarpaulin stretched tight and lashed to the body. The Negro driver leaned against the front fender and watched me come with a tight sick expression.

I showed him the badge and he looked at it without eagerness. A few drops of rain were falling. The shoulders of the road were already soft from a rain the night before.

"What happened?"

He waved his hand at the ditch on the opposite side. "That car came roarin' at me ninety miles a second. Straight at me, officer. I pulled clean off the road and he pulled out, too. I never heard such a noise. He musta laid down fifty feet of rubber. He went into that soft shoulder and couldn't bring it back. Went nose down into that ditch. Not more'n half a minute ago."

"Anybody hurt?"

His throat moved darkly as he swallowed. "I don't know. I'm afraid to go and look. He went over with an awful *whump*. I thought I saw one of 'em throwed out."

I swore to myself. "All right. You got a flashlight in that rig?"

"Yes, sir."

"Get it and stand back of my car. If anybody comes along slow him down. I'll go down and count the pieces."

He walked toward the cab of the truck, his feet heavy.

"Oh, God," he moaned. There was more rain, falling straight down, silently.

I went to my car, a '53 Oldsmobile, the down payment on which I had paid out of what I had saved buying clothes at Starkey's, got a slicker from the back seat and a flashlight from the dash compartment. I crossed the highway and started down the steep slope of the ditch.

There was a woman in slacks lying face up on the bank about halfway into the ditch. Her face was bloodless. I kneeled beside her and let the light play over her. She was out cold, but nothing seemed to be broken. Her breathing was all right.

I turned my light on the car, a new black Chrysler, wedged in at the bottom of the ditch between the two steep sides. The light fell on a man leaning against the side of the Chrysler, holding his stomach with one hand. There was a dark cut on his forehead.

I walked up to him, holding the light in his face. He was good-looking, with lean jaws and heavy eyebrows and a wide mouth. His gray eyes were dulled from fright or pain. I recognized him right away.

"Hurt?" I asked him.

"Steering wheel caught me in the gut," he said carefully, as if he wasn't quite sure he would be able to talk without pain. "Not too hard. Knocked the wind out of me. I think I cut my head."

"You did. It doesn't look bad." I stepped closer to him. He was breathing with his mouth open, and I could smell the whiskey he had been tucking away. He didn't look drunk, though.

"That's some breath you got there," I said. "It should go point one five on the drunkometer, easy."

"Who are you?" he said suspiciously.

"Sergeant Randall, Cheyney police."

"Jesus," he said sardonically, "am I lucky tonight." He still held his stomach. "Why don't you go away and let somebody else rescue me?"

"How fast were you traveling, hot rod?"

"Too fast. I know. Listen, I'm not drunk. I've had a couple, but I'm not drunk. I could handle the car. I could handle it all right. It was the soft shoulder that did the damage."

"Yeah."

His voice strengthened as he became angry. "Hell, nobody was hurt, so why make a fuss?"

"You ought to see the look on the face of that colored boy you almost ran down. Ask him why the fuss. Ask the lady. She's not taking a nap up there."

He seemed almost disgusted. "She got panicky when we started to slide. Jerked the door open and bailed out. She probably passed out when she hit, that's all."

His forehead was wrinkled. He passed a hand over his eyes and straightened up uncertainly. He took his hand away from his belly and nothing fell out so he turned around and leaned into the car and took something off the front seat. It was a half-full fifth of whiskey.

As he brought it up I reached out and took it away from him, put it in my raincoat pocket. He seemed about thirty years old or so but he looked like a kid when he got indignant.

"The driver's license," I said.

He leaned against the side of the car again. "I guess it's time for you to learn something," he told me, with a smug look in his eyes that said I was sure going to fall over when I heard it.

"I know," I said. "You're Nathan Hale Fisher, you're a selectman of Cheyney Township, and you're liable to be Works Commissioner come next election. And also your family is a big deal in these parts."

His face sagged a little as I spoiled his surprise. He rubbed a hand over his slack jaw. "Wait a minute. I'm a little fuzzy here. What was that name again?"

"Randall."

"You the detective was in charge of that Smithell mess?"

"The same."

He nodded gloomily. "Sure. Listen. I know it by heart. 'Well, I noticed lights on over at the Smithell house. It was about midnight, I guess. I thought he hadn't gone to bed. I was worried about the ring my wife had given me, so I . . .'

Will you please give me my bottle back for a second before you impound it?"

"Sure." I took the bottle out of my raincoat pocket, pulled the cork and let the whiskey spill out on the ground. He reached for it but I held the bottle out of the way until it was empty. Then I gave it to him. He took it with a sort of sneer and threw it away.

He put a hand on the fender of his car. "Now how the hell am I going to get this out of here?" he said. Falling rain had plastered his black hair against his forehead.

"Don't you think we ought to see about the lady?"

He blinked. His eyes were full of some terrible pain. "Leave her alone," he said, with weary unconcern. "She's no better than the mud she's lying in."

I looked at him for a few seconds. He was grinding his back teeth together. He held one hand tight to his temples. "Pickup?"

"Yeah. Yeah. I found her in one of Roxy's joints."

"You know Roxy Marko?"

He held up two fingers together. "Like this," he said.

I turned away from him and walked up the bank toward the woman, slipping some in the mud. The rain had brought her to and she looked up at me, scared, her face and hair sodden, her slacks tight on her legs. She moaned, front teeth edging over her underlip.

"You all right, lady?"

"I'm dying," she said. "I'm dying."

"Why don't you try to get up?" I said. She smelled worse than Fisher.

"No," she said. "I'm dying."

"Come on," I said. "This is no place for it. Come on and get up."

"I got a pain," she said. She put her hand on her abdomen. "I got a pain here."

"I hope it's a boy," I said politely.

At this, she moved around and lurched to her feet like a colt learning to walk. She had hair only a little darker than orange peel and a sagging chin and pouches under her eyes. She looked about thirty-five.

"Goddam sonbitch," she muttered, shivering. "Gon' sue goddam sonbitch drive so fast." She slipped and fell against me, legs dragging. "I'm dying."

I picked her up and carried her out of the ditch, placing my feet carefully on the slippery bank. I carried her across the road and tucked her away in my Oldsmobile. On the floor of the back seat. I didn't want my seat covers ruined. She was due to puke her head off.

It was raining harder as I climbed back down the bank. Fisher was still beside his car. He stood there in the rain with water dripping from his hair, his forehead lined with pain, his teeth chattering. He looked bad.

He put his hands over his handsome face. "Ah, God," he wailed. "I've got another damned headache." He took his hands away and turned toward the car and took three steps alongside it, then slipped in the mud. He kneeled beside the back fender and looked at me as if I had interrupted his evening prayer.

"What are you looking at?" he cried, his eyes squinting and wild. "Like fingers squeezing my head . . . What are you looking at, you dirty son of a bitch?" He got to his feet and floundered around the car and jerked open the front door, half-fell into the front seat, reached out a hand to open the glove compartment. He groped inside. Rain hit against the roof and made a loose wet curtain covering the door space. His feet scrambled a little on the ground. He took out a small bottle, uncapped it, and white pills gleamed in his muddy palm. He swallowed them, put his face against the seat in a vise formed by his arms. He stayed that way for about a minute, then slipped out of the car, turned his head and vomited. It lasted a long time, or maybe it just seemed long, standing in the rain. Finally he crawled away from his regurgitation and lay down in a cradle of wet weeds. I went over to him and took him by the shoulder. His face was composed. The vomiting seemed to have done him some good. One of his eyes, the one I could see, opened a little.

"Take me home," he said.

So I went out of the ditch again. The truckman stood in

the road, his flashlight pointed at the blacktop.

"Wasn't nobody hurt much, was they?" he said.

"No," I said. "I need some help now. I have to haul out a man. I don't think I can manage by myself."

He came with me, walking behind me. "I should have gone down in the ditch, I know it," he said apologetically. "Everybody's afraid of something. I guess I'm just most afraid of seein' hurt people."

"You think I'm afraid of something?" I said.

"Why," he said surprised, "why, I don't know."

The hell he didn't. He could smell it on me, like a dog can. But he couldn't know why, and I didn't know, myself.

3

THE GIRL who looked out at me had straight black hair, cut very short, expressive blue eyes, and a small mouth. Her face was narrower than most, but she was a tall girl and it looked all right. Her breasts rose high and pointed, under some kind of black skintight pullover sweater without sleeves. She was Nathan Fisher's sister, and she was very beautiful. She frowned slightly at me as if she couldn't quite remember where she had known me, and wanted to remember.

"Yes?"

"I'm Sergeant Bill Randall." I explained myself.

"Why . . . yes." She smiled at me, a good sort of mischievous smile as if we were sharing a racy secret. "You were in charge of"—a shadow over the shrewd smiling blue eyes—"Mr. Smithell's murder."

"The investigation. That's right."

The door opened more. Her legs were long and slimly curved, revealed by high-cut white shorts. "Come in, Sergeant. What can I do for you?"

"Thank you. It's about your brother."

"Nathan?" I noticed the tightening of her long trim fingers around the doorknob, the quick uncertain change of tone in her voice.

"Yes. He—he was in an accident." Goddam, Bill, quick before she passes out. "I mean, it was nothing serious. He's not hurt. He was driving a little fast and hit a soft shoulder. I happened to be around. I brought him home. He's asleep in my car."

She had sagged momentarily against the door. Now she straightened, stood tall in front of me. A smile fluttered. "Oh," she sighed.

"I'm sorry," I said. "I was clumsy about telling you. I always am with these things."

"That's all right." The smile was firm, and for me. "Shall we get Nathan out of your car? It's not raining so hard now."

"I think it's just about stopped."

I stood aside as she walked through the big door. She was slim and tall and I admired the sleek long movements of her legs. Her walk was spoiled somewhat by a limp. But I noticed that her bad ankle had become a lot better since the night of the Smithell murder.

The light went on when I opened the car door and she leaned inside, her lips parting in a grimace as she saw the cut over Nathan's eye. She looked over the front seat at the woman sprawled in the back and then again at Nathan almost immediately, her eyes empty. She raised one hand and touched fingers to the dried cut. Her face was gentle. She took him by the shoulder and shook him lightly.

"Nathan. Nathan!"

His eyes came open some and he looked at her. His mouth formed a loose smile. "Umm," he said. "Hi." He settled a little more in the front seat and closed his eyes again and went back to sleep.

She looked back at me, helplessly.

"I'll carry him," I said.

Upstairs I sat Nathan on the edge of his bed and Karis Fisher deftly undressed him. He was half awake, offered no help or resistance. She coaxed him into his pajamas and we put him to bed. Then she took a damp cloth from the adjoining bathroom and sponged his face. She didn't seem upset by her brother's condition. I guessed this was not the first time she had seen him that way.

I looked around his bedroom, noting the single bed. I remembered the heavy square ring that Fisher wore. His wife had given Nathan that ring, the ring he had left in a bathroom of Leland Smithell's house the night Smithell had been killed, which was why he returned to the Smithell house and discovered the man's body.

"What about his wife?" I asked.

She looked at me, her eyes frightened. "What about—who?"

"Nathan's wife. The one who gave him the ring. Are they . . ."

"Oh," she said, relieved. "You mean Kelly Anne. I thought you were talking about . . . that thing in the car. That would have been going too far." She finished adjusting the covers about him, bent and kissed his forehead ligtly. "Even for Nathan."

She took the washcloth into the bath, began turning out lights. I waited in the hallway for her as she closed the door carefully.

"Nathan's wife died about a year ago," she said. "Right here in the house, during some silly little party. Kelly Anne had a very bad heart and everybody knew it. She was right in the middle of a drink and she just folded up. Dr. Einhorn was here, too. He'd been treating her. He said she was probably dead before she hit the floor. Too much strain or something. Her heart failed. Nathan was grief-stricken. He loved her very much. I'm afraid he didn't get much love back. I guess Kelly Anne was all right in her way. A flashy type blonde, stunning figure. She just didn't care much about anything except Kelly Anne."

There was a gleam of dislike in her eye, dislike that apparently hadn't softened any with the passing of a year.

"Should she have been drinking if she had a heart condition?"

"No, but that was Kelly Anne for you. She said a bad heart wasn't going to make an invalid of her. She carried on as if she had a spare one in her purse. Nathan worried himself sick about her. He gave her a lot of love. I don't know what she gave him. I guess I couldn't understand." At the top of the stairs she turned to me. "Maybe you think I'm not upset when Nathan's like that. But I am. Nathan's really a fine man. He has a promising career ahead. He . . . just gets tired, sometimes." Her chin trembled a little. "I guess I should be glad it doesn't happen more often. I wish he would forget her. I wish he would."

"Don't you think he needs a doctor? He complained about a headache."

"No. I wouldn't bother Dr. Einhorn about it. Nathan needs sleep more than anything else. He has those headaches now and then. He works far too hard. He's running for Works Commissioner in the fall, you know. Sometimes he goes over forty hours without rest. That contributes as much as anything to his . . . lapses. Maybe when the elections are over things will become more normal."

"I guess it's none of my business, but this sort of thing isn't so good for him politically."

Her eyes were troubled. "Do you think that woman—"

"I doubt if she's aware of who he is. He's liable to get hold of a smart one some day, though, who would talk to anybody for the right price. That would be bad."

"I know, I know," she said miserably. "I can't predict what Nathan will do next. I try to look after him, make him take time out for golf, or just loafing. He doesn't really care about drinking. He just . . . has to. It must be lonely for him, despite his public life. We live here alone, since mother died about a year and a half ago. But Nathan and I were raised in this house and I hate to give it up."

We stood less than a foot apart, sharing a comfortable feeling of intimacy undisturbed by an awareness of being strangers.

"It must be lonely for you, too."

She sat on the top step, patted the carpet beside her. I sat down, too.

"No, not really. There's always something to do in Cheyney or up at State. Parties and weddings. I guess I have the usual number of boy friends."

"But no one in particular?"

She gave me a curious glance. "No. There never has been. Later, maybe. Right now there's Nathan to think about."

"You're not still in college?"

"No. I graduated two years ago. I went to Smith my first year—" She smiled. "Mother insisted. Both she and grandmother graduated from Smith. But I was homesick and I got tired of all those Ivy League types. I finished up at State."

The sadness seemed to have left her. "Would you like some coffee?"

"No, thanks, Miss Fisher, I . . ."

She tugged at my hand. "Come *on*," she said urgently. "And don't call me Miss Fisher. My name's Karis. It's sort of silly, but that's what mother wanted."

"I like it," I said, smiling a little. "Just one cup, and I'll go."

I followed her down the stairs. She walked carefully, favoring her injured ankle, supporting herself with one hand on the banister. Near the bottom of the stairs I put my hands around her waist and lifted her the rest of the way down.

"Ah," she said, "muscles."

"Yeah. That ankle still pretty bad?" I asked, embarrassed a little.

"It's coming along. What a whack I gave it!"

"How did it happen?"

"Right after Nathan discovered Mr. Smithell was dead he came running back here. He yelled up to me from the front hallway. I thought the house was on fire, or something, so I threw on a robe and came running. My legs got all tangled up somehow and I hit my ankle against the banister post at the top of the stairs. I thought I'd die. That was a bad night for me. Seeing Mr. Smithell dead like that after we had just left him. It makes me feel morbid thinking about it. And that boy. I heard he hanged himself."

"Yes."

She shook her head dolefully. "I heard it on the radio. The whole news broadcast was depressing. This is just one of those gloomy nights. I'm glad you happened along, Bill. Kitchen's this way."

She took me by the hand and smiled at me. I was glad I had happened along, too.

But why all the confiding in me? Why so friendly? I'm not that pretty.

"Maybe I ought to skip the coffee. That woman in the car is pretty sick," I said.

Karis dropped my hand.

ACCORDING TO AN ID CARD IN HER WALLET, WHICH SHE WORE attached to the belt of her slacks, the woman lived in an apartment on Foster Street, one block from the Katy yards. I took her there and shook her awake and guided her out of my car and up two flights of stairs, supporting her when she got the staggers. She chirped and cooed and giggled and moaned all the way.

When I got her inside her door she sat down on the floor with her feet sticking out in the hall and I couldn't talk her into getting up. I should have left her like that. Instead I picked her up and carried her into the bedroom.

I sat her on the bed and she got up immediately and went for the bathroom like somebody had pulled the cork. I noticed that there were signs of a man living with her.

When she came back she was wearing only the soggy sweater. She collapsed on the bed and got comfortable.

"I'm all weak," she said. "All weak. Undress me."

I took hold of the sweater with some reluctance and pulled and wrenched and tugged and it came off. I hung it over the back of a chair.

"You're nice to me," she said. "He wasn't nice. He prop-as-uh-properishuned me."

"A sweet kid like you," I said. "Imagine."

I put her head on the pillow and pulled a sheet over her. She opened her eyes and giggled, wrapped her arms around my neck.

"Hee, hee, hee," she said. "He's not nice, like you. Get in with me?"

"Some other time," I said.

But she found the strength to pull my head down and she kissed me on the nose, her mouth closing over the tip of it.

Hearing a noise, I removed the arms and straightened up. I turned toward the doorway. A man was standing there. A large man wearing denims, a khaki shirt. Hair puffed out at the throatline. His thick forearms were covered with it.

"He took my pants off me, Harry," the dame said, to get us off to a lively start. Hee, hee, hee.

"Who are you?" he said mildly.

"Detective Sergeant Bill Randall," I said, grinning foolishly. "The little lady was in an auto accident. I brought her home."

He looked from me to her. She had turned over on her stomach and seemed to be asleep.

"Well, I guess I'll be going." I walked toward the door. He stepped aside without looking at me. "That's quite a girl," I said, just to be saying something.

"You ought to be married to her," he said quietly, without turning his head.

"Hee, hee, hee," the redhead giggled, the sound of it muffled because her face was in the pillow.

I MADE IT MY BUSINESS TO CALL ON NATHAN FISHER THE next morning. He had a couple of small rooms in the Times Publishing Company building above the pressroom. I went through an outer door with a long ugly crack in the glass like a sudden pain and found myself looking at a young man with waved blond hair and pale blue eyes who sat behind a secretary's desk in one corner of the room.

He had a flat briefcase in his lap and a .38 caliber revolver in a holster under one arm. I couldn't see the gun but I knew the man and knew he always carried it.

His name was Walsh and he looked after Dan Campion, who had been governor of the state a number of years ago, then a senator in Washington. Campion was after another term as governor, which was probably the reason for his visit to Nathan, who was in line for nomination as State Works Commissioner on the Campion ticket.

Walsh nodded my way. "Randall."

"Hello, Walsh. How long has that been going on?"

He looked toward the door of Nathan's office. Campion's pale silhouette moved over the glass as he walked restlessly around inside.

"All morning." A twist of his arm gave him the time, and he frowned slightly. "They're about due to break it up. Dan's got a lunch date over in Wescott in forty-five minutes." He looked at me amiably through the smoke from a cigarette. "You come to see Dan's boy?"

I nodded. The voices of the two men inside were audible but muffled. "Strategy meeting?" I said.

"Big rally up in Kell County, the twenty-third. Dan's charting the plays."

"How does Nathan stack up in this state?" I said.

Walsh shrugged. "I don't need to tell you about politics, do I? Nathan works hard, he has that certain flair that makes votes stick to him. He's sincere, but he doesn't let that get in the way of ambition. The only drawback is, he's young. Mr. East and Mr. West like their boys more mature and not so gung ho. But Campion's softening them up. If he brings those two around, Nathan's got it knocked. He'll be right next door to the big office before you know it. He'll learn a lot from Dan up there. I'd say things look good for him, if he doesn't pull a fruitcake somewhere."

"Yeah," I said. Walsh was watching me with his customary eager-beagle look, his face still and alert, as if he was waiting for me to say something more. The door from Nathan's office opened suddenly, diverting Walsh's attention. He swung out of his chair easily.

Nathan and Dan Campion came out. They both nodded, but Nathan seemed too absorbed in something Campion was saying to pay much attention to me. After the ex-governor and Walsh had left, Nathan stared at me a moment, then said, "Come on inside, Randall."

I went. Nathan's office was furnished simply, with a second-hand desk that needed varnish, a few chairs and a large filing cabinet. There was a framed picture of his sister on the desk.

Nathan offered me a cigarette, took one for himself. I looked him over critically. His face was carefully shaved, but his eyes were watery and tired.

"How're you feeling?" I said.

He snorted and managed a smile, blinked at smoke that hovered near his eyes. "Like my joints are eggshell. Big rag rug in my mouth." He drew on the cigarette, looked at it with distaste and flipped it into an empty wastebasket.

"We hauled your car out of the ditch," I said. "Minor damage. You can claim it in the garage back of the jail. Cost you five dollars for towing."

He nodded gloomily, seemed to think about it a moment. He swung around to face me with a quizzical smile.

"I don't remember a whole lot about last night. You looked after that girl—?"

"I took her home. She wasn't hurt. She was no girl, either."

"Ummmhumm," he said, as if it wasn't important. Maybe it wasn't. "She could have been sixteen, for all I could tell. Those lights in the place. No lights, actually. Ought to pass a law about places like that. Too easy to pick up. Too easy to get picked up. I don't know. She just didn't seem bothered when I puked under the table. That impressed me. I wasn't drunk. Just some bad beer. Hell of an evening."

The words rambled out with no particular thought or inflection behind them, as if his mind was rewinding after the session with Campion. He irritated me slightly, but at the same time I felt in touch with him emphatically, as if I could know his moods and desires without understanding them. Nathan had a magnetic quality, all right. A politician.

"You keep diversified company," I said. "You hop from a tavern broad to the ex-governor of the state in a matter of hours and the only change I can see in you is a clean shirt."

He smiled as if I had hurt him. "I don't intend to do it. I know what I should do and what I shouldn't. But up comes this thing and carries me off and the part of me that knows better can't help me."

"Your kind of mistake is the kind you can make too often."

He accepted that. He sat on the edge of his desk and watched the fingers of his right hand curl and uncurl. "I'm beautiful this morning," he said with faint irony. "I'm really beautiful this morning." He looked at me again. "Am I going to have any court trouble because of that creature last night?"

"No."

"You reading me off with a warning?"

"I don't know what else to do with you."

"Yeah." He studied his hands. "I won't do it again," he said. They were just so many words.

"Take care of yourself," I said. "Take care of your sister."

I went out and shut the door behind me.

I WAS AT MY CLUTTERED DESK IN POLICE HEADQUARTERS about midnight when Phil Naar poked his head in the door.

"You still hanging around?" I said. Phil was working the 3-11 that week.

He came inside. He was wearing a coffee-colored shirt, sticking wet to him in places. He rested his stocky body in a chair near the window and gave me a tired grin.

"We had a cutting down in the Mill Bottom," he said. "Two kids were arguing over what to play on the juke box, for Christ's sake." He patted his face and neck with his handkerchief. "I been over to St. Kit's with it."

"How did you get that?" I said, noticing the bandage on his left hand.

"A little trouble getting one of the kids into the squad car. The one that was still standing when we got there. He bit me. Smith had to unload his billy on the boy before we could handle him. Kids!"

"Yeah."

He looked at the folder and pictures on my desk. "What have you got there? Jimmy Herne?"

I nodded. "I was adding the newspaper clippings about his suicide. Should I send out for coffee?"

"I can't drink coffee in the summer. I must have told you that before."

"Must have. It's just my age. I can't remember what people tell me any more. Old ladies help *me* across the street."

"Send that to Jerry. He could use it."

Jerry was Phil's boy. He had a local television program out in Hollywood and played bit parts in movies.

"On second thought," Phil said, "I'll tell him myself when I get out there." He looked at a calendar on one wall. "My God, eight more months. Only eight more months and then forty-four dollars and seventy-six cents a week for the rest of my life. All that, and social security, too."

He reached out and unlaced his shoes, let them drop on the floor. His feet were on the radiator, which hasn't worked for years. I don't mean to sound like we're hard up. The roof doesn't leak, unless somebody spits on it.

"I heard something real interesting," I said. "According

to Miller Starkey, Jimmy Herne was telling the truth about where he got the thirty dollars."

Phil picked at something stuck between a couple of his teeth. "You planning to let Gulliver know?" he said, trying to sound disinterested.

"I already did."

He put his feet on the floor. "What did he say?"

I grinned. "He said I spoiled his evening."

Phil spoke morosely. "The way you keep sticking your head in that lion's mouth fascinates me. Either you got more guts than good sense or else you're trying to prove something to yourself."

I quit smiling. "Like what?"

"Aw," Phil grumbled, "how would I know? You're the college boy." He didn't look at me.

"The college boy," I repeated. "Maybe that bothers you. Maybe you think you should be giving the orders around here."

"Cut it out," Phil said sharply. "I'm not the executive type. I'm just the kind of guy who spends his life taking orders and doing the best he can. I know that. It doesn't make any difference to me."

We stared at each other for a while, not hostilely, but grimly. I broke it up. "Sorry, Phil. I've been touchy lately for some reason."

He turned a little and stared out of the window. I tucked the papers on my desk into Jimmy's folder. The photos remained spread out on my blotter. I looked at them again. I had taken them myself and they showed good detail. Three of the pictures were of Leland Smithell lying on the rug in his living room. He was wearing an undershirt and trousers, his bare feet were in slippers. The candy dish, of hammered copper with a wooden handle, lay on the floor nearby. It had been used to kill Smithell. The back of his head was badly crushed. He had been hit at least twice, and the autopsy surgeon reported that the back of his skull had collapsed, shoving pieces of bone into the brain.

The first blow possibly had only stunned him, and he had stumbled against an end table near the sofa, upsetting the heavy metal table lamp, which could be seen on the floor in the pictures.

Along with several diagrams of the first floor of the house, I put the pictures back in the folder. Impulsively, I took out my report of the investigation and Jimmy's confession, re-read them both.

Smithell had lived in Cheyney about three years. No one knew where he was from, and apparently he had no living relatives. A check of his few papers turned up no letters from anywhere but Cheyney. He wasn't wealthy but had enough money to invest in the expansion program of Nordin Kaylor, and eventually became Kaylor's partner. He lived in a new ranch-type house just down the street from the Fishers in the best section of town, apparently lived quietly. He entertained occasionally, belonged to Wood Hills Country Club and was socially acceptable. He seemed about fifty years old. His only charity had been a homely kid named Jimmy Herne, whom he had heard about from a friend connected with the state prison system. He had wanted someone to look after his house for him, and Jimmy eventually got the job. Somebody, besides Stella Francis, had been hoping Jimmy would straighten out. But Jimmy murdered Smithell, prob-ably without meaning to, for a couple of rings and other pieces of men's jewelry. And, apparently, thirty dollars. He had never had a chance to get away with it and he had finally ended his unattractive life personally, after confessing. There was nothing more.

Nothing more, except that I couldn't quite think of Jimmy as just another folder filled with reports and fingerprint cards and arrest sheets. Maybe that was Stella's fault, for trying to make me see the hard ugly life when nobody gives a damn. So that I had to think about a frightened kid walking away from the reformatory, telling himself, grimly, that he was through with it, that he'd die before he went back.

Then staying with Stella a while, before the job with Smithell came along.

Washing dishes, cutting grass, catering to and supervising routine for an aging bachelor.

For ten months. And then . . .

A mistimed try for quick money, and running.

And being brought back, and knowing there wasn't a chance, because nobody would listen to him.

Phil was still looking out of the window, and I wondered if he was remembering, as I was . . .

The kid lay beside the wooden chair in the basement, the chair that was bolted to the floor. Gulliver lifted his head with a hand under the chin.

"I . . . didn't . . . do . . . it . . ."

Gulliver looked at Phil Naar, who had come in quietly while it was going on. I watched both of them.

"Clean him up, Phil, and take him over to the jail." Gulliver went to the door and left without looking again at Jimmy Herne.

Phil wet his handkerchief at a sink on the wall. He helped Jimmy to a sitting position. Jimmy's head hung, as if he didn't have strength to lift it. Blood was bright on Jimmy's lower lip. Phil wiped at it with the handkerchief.

"You must have bit your lip," he said.

He helped Jimmy to his feet. The kid stood uncertainly for a moment, finding strength. He held his head gently with his hands.

"I guess I don't need to put the cuffs on you just to walk over to the jail, do I?" Phil said.

Jimmy turned and kicked him. It seemed to take all he had because he sat down then, in the chair.

"What . . . did you do that for?" Phil said, his eyes full of hurt. "I didn't do anything to you."

Jimmy sobbed. "You goddam cop!"

"You got a cigarette, Bill?"

"Oh? Sure." I tossed him my pack and he lit one.

"Thanks. Well, I guess I ought to go on home. No reason to stick around. No reason for you to stick around, either."

"No." I put the remaining papers in the folder, secured it. "What do you think, Phil? I mean about Jimmy and the thirty dollars."

Phil sighed, and began putting on his shoes. "There had

to be some truth in him somewhere. I guess that was it."

"Suppose that wasn't all the truth."

He gave me a frayed stare. "What do you want to say, Bill?"

"Damned if I know."

Phil stood up and took out his handkerchief, patted his chin. "Eight more months," he said, to himself. "Just eight more months. I don't want to do anything but stay out of his way for that long. I don't even want him to know I'm around, for eight more months."

His face was drawn. There was a sour tension in the hot little room, and I knew he could taste it. He sighed. "Well, there's always the chance we were wrong about . . ."

"Suppose we don't talk about it," I said. "Suppose we forget all about it because we can't do anything about it anyway, now."

Phil took his hat off, combed his slack white hair with his fingers and put the hat back on.

"If you find a way to forget it," he said irritably, "let me know. I'd like to get some sleep too."

4

THREE NIGHTS later I was going into my office when the desk officer looked my way and said, "Can you come here a minute, Sergeant?"

I went behind the railing. He thumbed down the button on the radio mike and said, "Will you give me that again, Russ? Sergeant Randall's standing by."

Russ was in one of our three cars. "We just drove past the Smithell house, Sergeant," he said over the loudspeaker. "Isn't the place supposed to be locked up?"

"It is locked up," I said. "Why?"

"We saw a light. Just for a second, at one of the front windows. Like a flashlight somebody was being careful with."

"No mistake?"

"Now, Bill . . ." he sounded pained.

"Okay. Who's with you? Concannon?"

"Sure."

"If somebody's inside, I don't want you all barging in on him. Just make sure he stays inside until I get there. Understand?"

"I get it," he said briskly. "I'll take the front and Con will watch the back door."

"Don't go waving that gun of yours around," I said. "It may just be a real estate man showing the house to a prospective buyer. Or something."

"Sure," Russ said, with a wink in his voice.

I went into the office and took my gun and belt holster from the desk. If you like fast hard-hitting hand guns, you'd like mine. It's a Smith and Wesson .45 revolver, with the barrel cut down to four inches and a ramp sight mounted

for more maneuverability on the hip. The front of the trigger
guard is cut out, the butt rounded off and the hammer filed
down, all for a faster draw. Not that I usually need my gun
that fast. But you only have to be slow once to be dead.

I took the front door key of the Smithell house from the
bulletin board and went downstairs to my car.

Four minutes later I parked across the street from the
darkened Smithell house. The squad car was parked in a
driveway down the street, partially hidden behind a hedge.

Russ stepped out of the shadows between two trees near
the porch as I approached. "Nobody's come this way," he said
cheerfully, his voice low.

"Any more lights?"

"No."

"Let's go inside."

I tried the front door, found it locked. I unlocked it
quietly, swung the door open. It was black as the pitch of
hell inside. Light sprayed on the floor as I thumbed the button on my flash. I moved the light around, covering the
foyer, living room and dining room from where I stood.
Russ breathed heavily at my shoulder.

"Well," he said, scratching his belly comfortably. "I guess
we—*Jesus!*"

We both took a step backward at the sound of the scream
from within the house, wincing at the withering terror reflected in it, and the sound seemed to crawl right up my back
like something alive.

"What-in-the-hell . . ." Russ began. A second scream cut
him off.

With the flash moving the darkness out of the way ahead
of me, I ran through the dining room toward the kitchen
and the cellar stairs. The house was silent now except for
the memory of the last shocking scream and the heavy sounds
of Russ as he followed me.

I went down the stairs into the basement without bothering
to turn on the lights. When I hit the basement floor I let
the beam of light travel along the walls and Russ did the
same with his flashlight. We found what we were looking for
at the same time.

The girl in the doorway of the utility room turned a little as both flashlights concentrated on her. The edges of her blonde hair looked white against the darkness beyond the door. I didn't realize who I was looking at for a moment. She was wearing a green dress without sleeves, trimmed in white, with large white buttons. She had a flashlight, too, a small one, and in that caught moment that did not seem to be a part of time at all the flashlight slipped from her hand and hit the tiled floor, the glass shattering.

She moved then, almost drunkenly, one arm coming up to cover her eyes from the glare. Her mouth was open in an ugly way and her eyes were gone, brother, 'way gone. She took a couple of weaving steps and pitched forward but I knew it was going to happen and was there to catch her.

As I eased Stella to the floor there came a pounding at the basement door that led outside and Concannon was yelling something I couldn't catch. Russ yelled back at him and went clumping up the stairs to turn the lights on. Russ came back down swearing to himself, and hustled over to let Concannon in. The two of them looked in bewilderment at the girl on the floor.

I inclined my head toward the doorway from which Stella had come. "One of you take a look in there."

Russ went in with his gun and was about five seconds. He came back stabbing at his holster with the big revolver, a sick sheepish look on his face.

"Well," he said, "I guess we know what she was screaming about. Have a look, Bill."

I went in there. Behind me, Russ was saying, "You know, I think I had too much garlic in the spaghetti tonight. I'm afraid I'm going to be . . ." He made a rush for outdoors and was, on the grass.

I didn't blame him. Against one wall of the utility room was a trunk, the lid up. I looked inside. The man who looked back hadn't seen anybody lately. Not quite some time. And he didn't smell that way because he needed a bath.

I marched outside and leaned on the doorway. With some surprise I found my right hand had a death grip on the cut-down .45. I didn't remember drawing. I replaced the revolver and got myself a cigarette. My hand was shaking and I didn't give a damn who knew it.

"Somebody dead in there?" Concannon said. He's an ex-marine about five feet eight inches tall and at least that wide. He's put together as strongly as suspension cable, too.

"I'll say." I tilted my hat back and looked at Stella, lying on the floor. This part of the basement was a sort of party room, with paneled walls and a patterned tile floor. There was a lot of crazy metal furniture, too, and a small bar. Part of one wall was glass and there was a stone-paved patio outside, along with a hillside rock garden, barbecue pit and a gradually sloping lawn to the garage, the roof of which could be seen just inside the illumination provided by a couple of powerful floodlights mounted upstairs. These had been turned on by the same switch that worked the basement lights.

"How about getting some water for the lady?" I said. "Or would you rather go look at the body?"

"Not especially."

"The kitchen's upstairs to the right."

I went outside and told Russ to get my camera equipment out of the rear of my car and report in. I returned to the storage room and secured the lid before the air could go to work on him. There was no question as to how he had got it. About three-quarters of an inch of pointed steel poked through him just below the heart and his white shirt had turned rusty over a large area.

Concannon returned with some water and a couple of ice cubes wrapped in a tea towel. I turned my attentions to Stella. I kneeled on the floor and propped her against me, let ice water trickle over her face. Even though she was still out her face retained a look of strain, as if she hadn't been able to escape the sight of it even in unconsciousness.

The night was so hot the bugs were walking. There was a big wet spot on her dress in the hollow of her back. As she began to come around I sent Concannon upstairs to find out how she had got in.

Her eyes opened weakly and she looked up at me. For a second she didn't know me and then her lips closed over my whispered name and she struggled closer to me, one of her hands knocking my hat off as the arm looped around my shoulders.

"Bill," she whimpered. *"Bill!* Awful. In there. Awful."

"I know. I took a look."

"Bill, I've wanted to see you so bad. Why didn't you come to Jimmy's . . ."

"I wanted to come, Stella. Gulliver sent me out of town."

"How did you happen to . . ."

"You don't get to ask any more questions," I said. "My turn. What are you doing here?"

She looked puzzled for an instant, as if she didn't know what I meant. Then her breath caught jerkily and she reached toward her waist.

I rolled her off me and with a quick movement pinned both arms behind her, holding her wrists together with one hand.

"What are you doing, Bill!"

I slid my hand along her stomach and felt something hard under her dress. I pried two buttons loose. She twisted wildly as I reached beneath her dress.

"Bill, stop! What do you think—"

She whipped one arm free and tried to squirm away from me so I let go of her other arm and clamped my arm across her breasts, holding her fast. She got one hand high enough to be effective and I felt the sting of her fingernails. My hand closed around the object beneath her dress and I withdrew it, shook it free of the handkerchief in which it was wrapped. It hit in the stretched apron of dress between her spread legs and rolled to the floor. It was a round shiny compact with a small, jeweled design.

"Let go of me, you ——" she snapped, and the word hurt worse than her fingernails. I released her and she bent toward the compact, scooping it up with both hands. "The mirror's probably broken. Oh, thanks a lot!" She was almost in tears, but not only because of the compact.

"Whose compact is it?"

"Mine!"

"Where did you get it?"

She turned around so that she kneeled facing me. "I got

it here." Her face was splotched with color, glistened damply. Her eyes had a slanted hardness, and the closed mute look that betrayed her and all the others who knew their guilt. "That's why I came to get it. It's mine." She kept her voice low so she could control it.

"How did it get here?"

"I left it."

"When?"

"I don't know. A couple of months ago."

"When you were visiting Jimmy?"

She hesitated. I could hear the quick breathing in her throat. "No, I wasn't visiting Jimmy." There were tear streams on her face, but her eyes were defiant, and I thought I caught a glimpse of something basically vicious.

"I was visiting him."

"You mean Smithell?"

"Yes. Him. Smithell. Who do you think?"

"I don't know. Why?"

She laughed shakily. "Oh, you're smart tonight. You're so smart tonight. You know what for."

"I don't!"

She told me, in the crudest terms possible.

Funny little word, like a big swinging hammer, hitting with such force the impact is not truly realized at once. I reached out, my fingers locking tight about her arm. "You . . . you couldn't have. You . . ."

"Why not?" she said wildly. "Why not? You think he was too old? I can tell you he wasn't. I can tell you." She put her hands over her face to contain the bitter sobs.

I put the compact on the floor and backed away from her, retreating from the swing of the hammer and the crazy hurting. It was almost a minute before I realized my face was distorted in a grimace of disgust.

Concannon was standing close by. ". . . A window around by the side porch," he was saying. I barely heard him. "Probably left open a few inches. The screen wasn't hooked. She just lifted the window and crawled in that way. No breakage."

"Fine," I said, nodding, not knowing what I was saying.

"You've done a good job. Go wait in the car. I'll call you."

I looked down at her after he had gone, searching for the whore taint, trying to see her as she must be, as Gulliver and others saw her—Stella of the cheap carnal thrust of breast and teasing spread of pelvis. Far off, in a great gray place of mind, I heard my own inner voices trying to talk away the pain.

What did you expect? What? You knew it had to be like this. What did you expect, a padlock and sign, property of Bill Randall? What's the matter with you? You act like she was something, something. You dumb cop . . .

And above the undercurrent of reasoning the ugly fantasies rioted. I remembered the look of him, and while alive Smithell undeniably had had a certain hard gray handsomeness, his small body without flabbiness. It must not have been unpleasant for her.

Her crying had been brief and she was looking at me now, waiting carefully. She seemed uncertain of me, but her eyes showed no remorse. I knew then how it was with her, and me. Well, it didn't really matter. It wasn't important. I tried to think how to talk to her, how to be just as casual about it as she was.

"I . . . I . . . guess I . . . have been thinking kind of wrong about you."

Her lips parted and for an instant I thought I saw a hint of something in her eyes, deep hurt and loneliness. Then she picked up the compact and the green eyes were indifferent as she inspected her face in the mirror. She removed the pad from inside to touch up her face here and there.

"Don't let it get you down, Bill," she said unemotionally.

"Was the mirror broken?" I said. It seemed important.

"Cracked a little."

"What . . . did you do it for, Stella?"

She looked at me with a funny slanted smile, and I thought she was going to twist the knife deeper. Instead her features softened a little, and she said, "Bill . . . it was Jimmy. I made the mistake of .. . visiting him here one day. The old man wanted me. I knew, the way he looked at me. He came to my place and told me. He would open a savings account for

Jimmy. Every time I came to his bed he would put twenty-five dollars in the account for Jimmy." She paused, frowning a little. "I got took. He used me three times, told me not to come back. The part about the savings account . . ." She looked at me, cynical amusement in her eyes. "It wasn't true."

I saw now that maybe she was sorry, that she would try to make me believe it was all because of Jimmy and she hadn't enjoyed it a bit. I saw that.

"Just a whore job," I said roughly. "Just another whore job."

"Bill," she said, her voice tired. "Bill, please."

"Oh, yes," I said. "Don't let me offend you. Let's not talk about nasty things."

"What," she said, "do you want from me, Bill? Having a man doesn't mean much more to me than washing my hair." She grimaced in bewilderment. "All the time you keep trying to make me like I was something holy in a church."

"Shut up, you—"

I turned my back on her and went outside, into the night that simmered and was as sticky to move around in as wallpaper paste. I smelled the acrid vomit-stink deep in my nostrils and knew with a sort of harsh empty despair that I would always smell it when I thought of this time, and of her.

I threw a half-smoked cigarette into the grass and went back. She sat primly on the floor with her legs folded under her. Only the fingers laced tightly together in her lap betrayed her tension.

"You don't look good," I said. "Illegal entry, in the first place. Then there's that corpse in the trunk."

Her mouth pinched together and her face was old with the memory of shock.

"I'm going to be arrested," she said, with a thin sigh. "I know it. I expect it. Don't think you're telling me anything. But I just came to get what's mine. I didn't take anything else."

"Where was the compact?"

"In his bathroom. I had trouble finding it."

"How did you happen to get down to the basement?"

"I thought he might have something else of mine stored away. He was the souvenir-collecting type."

"Like what?"

"Oh . . . earrings or something. I'm not so rich I can afford to lose any."

"I'm sure you just walked out of here one night without them."

"You'd be surprised what a girl will do after . . ."

"Shut up."

"All right."

"You didn't find anything else?"

"Him." Her mouth twitched.

"Ever see him before?"

"Good Lord, no."

"Did you get a good look at him?"

"As good as I'm going to get. You couldn't force me to go back in there again and look. I'll die first."

"He was murdered, you know."

She looked at me calmly. "No. I didn't."

"How did you get in that storage room?"

"Walked in. Opened the door and walked in."

I glanced at the door. A padlock hung from a steep loop attached to the frame.

"You were being kind of brave, wandering around an empty house in the dark, weren't you?" I said.

"If I had known there were any dead men around I wouldn't have come within miles of the place," she replied. "I really wanted my compact back. It means . . . a great deal to me."

"For services rendered, no doubt."

"If it's all right with you, I'd like to go to jail now and get it over with," she said.

"Have you ever been booked before?"

"No." Hopefully, "Am I going to jail?"

"I don't know. Go over there and sit on that sofa until I'm ready to think about it."

She sat down and combed back her mane of hair with her fingers and folded her arms across her breasts. She stared silently at a clock on the opposite wall, waiting for the cuckoo to come out and wink at her.

I heard the sound of hard leather heels on the stone paving outside and Concannon said, "We've got a visitor, Sergeant."

I TURNED AND LOOKED AT KARIS FISHER. SHE WAS WEARING a robe, and moccasin slippers over her bare feet. She looked back at me timidly, her hands loosely clasped before her, like a chastened little girl. Concannon guided her respectfully inside with a hand at her elbow.

"Hello," I said, without enthusiasm.

"She was standing in the back yard next door," Concannon said, tilting his head in the direction of the house that stood between the Fisher home and Smithell's place, "looking down this way."

"I heard somebody screaming," Karis said irritably. "I didn't know you all were here. I thought . . . somebody should find out what happened. The Bishops are on vacation so I knew it didn't come from there. When I came across the Bishops' yard I saw a light in the basement here. Because of their hedge I couldn't see a police car or anything in the street. I was standing by the barbecue pit trying to decide what to do when this man came up behind me. He scared the life out of me."

Concannon looked at her wryly. "I'm sorry, lady. You scared me too." He reached to his belt and withdrew a .22 target pistol. "I didn't know she was carrying this. When she turned around the barrel wasn't more 'n six inches from me. My belly is still jumping.

"May I have it back now?" Karis said stiffly. Concannon glanced at me and I nodded. Karis took the automatic from his outstretched arm, jacked the shell out of the chamber, removed the magazine and let the slide forward, dropped the automatic into a pocket of her robe. She did this without looking at the gun. She looked around the basement alertly, noticing Stella. Her eyes rested on Stella for a few seconds, then turned toward me. Concannon touched the peak of his cap and went away.

"Did the scream wake you up?" I asked.

She seemed more relaxed now, but her eyes looked tired and there was a tight little stitch at one corner of her mouth. There was something about her that was very different from the Karis Fisher I had seen a few nights before. I realized then that the smile I had liked so much was necessary to counterbalance the slim dark brooding aspect of her. I wondered how I looked to her, what change was apparent since that swift fallen moment when Stella had challenged me to accept her cheapness.

"I wasn't sleeping," she said, her voice low. "I was standing at the window in my bedroom when I heard the scream. It was muffled, but enough to make me cringe. It made me want to hide under the bed. And at the same time I knew I had to find out."

She looked again at Stella.

"What is it, Bill? Who is this girl?"

"Stella Francis. Jimmy Herne's cousin. I can't tell you much yet. She found a dead man in that storage room." I indicated the open door.

"A . . . *dead man?*"

"A corpse," I said impatiently. "Dead. You know, not breathing."

She took a step toward the room.

"Better not. He's been in the trunk a long time. He looks like a dried green bean."

She slid back her foot uneasily and her shoulders pulled up slightly beneath the robe. "In the . . . who, Bill? Who is it?"

"How the hell would I know? He looks like practically nobody with his face the way it is."

She moved closer to me, and her eyes were on my cheek. She touched the rough drying scratches Stella had put there, until I took her hand away. I realized that she wasn't hurt by my rudeness, but in a few brief seconds had grasped a knowledge of me that I would never have been able to tell. I looked at her and her eyes were full of a fundamental strength and certainty, and shyness.

"Why didn't Nathan come?" I asked her.

She rubbed her forehead with her fingertips, her eyes

half-closed. "He . . . isn't home. He hasn't come home yet."
And I understood then the standing at the window, with
night shrinking around her, and the somber look of beginning
fear. It was part of the strengthening awareness we both
shared, that had begun at so strange and yet so proper a time.

"Bill," Stella said in a stricken voice.

I looked at her, startled. Her hands were over her face,
her legs pressed tightly together.

Karis went to her, putting a hand on Stella's shoulder.
Stella leaned away from her touch, the compact sliding off
her thigh, a polished glimpse of gold between folds of the
handkerchief.

Karis reached toward it, leaning over Stella, but Stella
grabbed it with both hands and stood up.

Karis spoke. "Bill—when you can, will you come and tell
me about it?"

"If you want me to."

She gave me a sad smile and left, the target gun hanging
heavy in one pocket of her robe.

Russ came clumping down the stairs with my camera
equipment. I told him where to stack it.

"Take Stella," I said to Russ.

"What do we book her on?"

Stella looked dully at me. Her mouth was open as if she
didn't have enough will to close it.

"We don't. You're taking her home, not downtown."

Russ looked at me questioningly. "Yes, sir," he said finally.
He had never called me "sir" in his life before.

Stella straightened and tugged at her dress. She held the
compact tightly in one hand. "Bill—" she said, her voice full
of despair.

"Get her out of here," I said. I bent over and picked my
hat off the floor, went back into the storage room.

The trunk was pushed up against a thin partitioning wall.
I opened a door in this wall and found that a furnace occupied most of the space on the other side. Water and steam
pipes ran close to the ceiling in the storage room.

Next to the trunk lay a suitcase with a corroded brass lock.
I noticed some bright scratches in the greenish corrosion,

which could indicate that the suitcase had been opened recently. Directly above the lock of the suitcase hung the L-joint of a water pipe, conspicuously new.

I found nothing inside when I opened the suitcase. But as I brushed my fingertips across the lining I discovered a small slit and a bulkiness underneath. Reaching inside the slit, I withdrew a handful of old newspaper clippings.

I spread some of them out on the concrete floor. One headline in particular caught my eye:

$40,000 STOLEN FROM INDUSTRIAL NATIONAL
BANK

IDENTIFYING THE MAN IN THE TRUNK WAS EASY. HIS POCKETS were clean; there was no wallet or anything like that. But the clothing labels had not been removed. We put out tracers and found that his name was Joseph Veilleux, and his last address 649 Darby Street, Troy, New York. He was forty-four years old, five feet nine inches tall, and weighed about one hundred sixty pounds when alive. There were also a couple of pictures which showed him to be a rather sullen-looking man with a thick mustache. The Troy police later sent us a photostat of an expired permit to carry a gun, partially explaining the .38 revolver we had found in his coat pocket.

I was tagging the revolver on my desk when Hugo Kenwick came into the office. Hugo is a grim-faced man with oily gray hair and many brownish splotches on his face. He is always washing his hands together as if something unpleasant clings to the skin. Hugo is a successful mortician and, due to the turn of a political card, our county coroner. We've had worse coroners. Hugo is conscientious about the job, and he has a son in medical school who helps him over the rough spots.

He tossed a couple of paper-clipped sheets of paper at me. "Here's the gory details," he said loudly. Hugo is a little deaf and hates to miss a word he says. He brushed at a couple of aphid-like insects on his soiled white shirt and added,

"God, between the bugs and the heat, how can you guys stand it in here?"

I looked at Phil Naar, who was over by the high open window, talking on the phone to someone at the Troy police department. He turned away slightly and put a finger in his other ear.

"We manage somehow," I said. I pushed Hugo's report aside and yawned. It had been a long night and I was beginning to feel the relaxation of pressures along with a sense of satisfaction, as the thing became explainable.

I picked a couple of bugs out of the hair on my forearms, said, "I don't have time to wade through all that, Hugo. Give me a summary."

The coroner settled back against the door frame, his damp hands feeling each other. "Well, he's been dead six months to a year. That's about as close as I can narrow it down."

"He's been dead nine months," I interrupted. "He checked into the Crown Hotel last October, stayed two days, checked out. He left his bag with the hotel people, but never came back for it. He disappeared completely. Into a trunk in Smithell's basement."

Hugo nodded. "The carving knife in him probably cut the hepatic vein. I can't be sure. There wasn't much to him. Just a dried bag of bones. Bacteria in the colon took care of his insides. Total decomposition was prevented because the trunk was in a nice dry place near the furnace. An interesting case of mummification."

Phil hung up the phone and came over to my desk. He flipped over a few pages of the pad he had been scribbling on, slipped on his reading glasses. Sweat drops clung to the underside of his bristly chin.

"Here's what I got," he said eagerly. "Veilleux was a guard at Industrial National Bank. Had been since 1937. He continued to work there after the embezzlement three-and-a-half years ago. Eight months later, after the hue and cry had died down, he quit his job. Said he was going into business for himself. Instead, he left Troy. Nobody there has heard a word from him since. He was the loner type, no close friends, lived simply. He wasn't acquainted with Olson other than to nod good-morning to him."

"Looks like he had a lead nobody else knew about," I said. "I guess we'll never find out what it was. So he left Troy, and patiently tracked Olson for almost three years."

"What was his angle?" Phil wondered. "Blackmail? Or did he want what was left of the loot for himself? If he wanted the reward money all he had to do was tip the FBI and let them do the work."

I shrugged. Hugo said, "Who did the job on this Veilleux?"

"Leland Smithell. That was the name he used in Cheyney. But Smithell was really Richard Olson, a minor vice-president with the Industrial National Bank in Troy, New York. He managed the theft of approximately forty thousand bucks and absconded. Bank officials didn't know about it for three days. The trail was cold when the FBI took over. The case is still open. At least, it was until tonight."

I handed Hugo some of the clippings Smithell had meticulously saved. "Compare those newspaper photos of Richard Olson with the pictures of Smithell. They don't look too much alike at first glance, but notice the shape of their heads, facial contours, the prominent ears. We phoned the FBI in St. Louis. They'll make the final decision."

Hugo nodded, looking at the pictures, then leafing through the newspaper accounts of the embezzlement.

"You think Veilleux tracked Smithell all the way to Cheyney?"

"Apparently. He may have threatened to expose Smithell if Smithell didn't pay off heavily. Smithell wouldn't give up his new life easily, after all the trouble he went to. He must have used the first weapon that was handy, a carving knife from the kitchen, and stuffed the body into that trunk. Then he discovered getting a body out of that neighborhood wouldn't be easy. So he left it where it was. The hot dry air in the basement through the winter kept the corpse from smelling very much. He kept the storage room locked. Veilleux was as safe from discovery there as he would be anywhere."

Hugo replaced the clippings and pictures on my desk. "Where'd you dig up these?"

"In a suitcase beside the trunk. The suitcase probably held the money at some time or other."

"Sort of a dead end after all, isn't it? With Smithell, uh, Olson, already dead?" Hugo looked at his watch. "Four-fifteen. Guess I'll say good night. I've already lost four hours' sleep on this thing." He put his hand in front of his face to stop a yawn and drifted out.

Phil, watching him leave, said, "That's one thing about Hugo. A simple explanation always makes him happy." He sat on the edge of my desk and picked up the match folder I had found in the storage room. " 'Quality Plumbers. No job too small or too large. We do only A-1 work.' So who gives a damn?" He dropped the match book back on the desk. "What did you find out from them, Bill?"

"One of their boys replaced that leaky L-joint which caused the corrosion on the lock. The work was finished a couple of days before Smithell was murdered," I said, trying to massage the ache from my eyes. "I talked with the plumber who made the repair. He said Smithell stayed with him every second, then locked the door carefully when he left. He also says there was no suitcase in the room."

"So it seems Smithell could have brought the money in the suitcase, then," Phil said. "I wonder how much?"

I put my hand on the folder containing Smithell's bank books and account statements—his financial history in Cheyney. "We've accounted for something less than twenty-six grand. You can start guessing from about fifteen thousand dollars on down."

"What do you think he did with that fifteen? He didn't make any deposits in either account during the two days between the plumber's visit and his death. Nordin Kaylor says business has never been better, so he didn't need quick money for any crisis there. Maybe there wasn't any money in the suitcase. Maybe he spent it long ago."

"Then he didn't need to hide the suitcase while the plumber was there. Unless on account of those press clippings. But why would he cache his press clippings in an otherwise empty suitcase? I think the man was an egoist. He'd want some of the money around where he could get it out and look at it now and then. Just to remind himself how clever he'd been. Like the clippings. Symbols of his master mind. He sure as hell didn't need to spend it. Not with the monthly dividends he received for his share of Kaylor's automobile business."

Phil chuckled, cleaned his glasses with a wrinkled handkerchief and put them away. There were heavy dark moons under his eyes. "Now you've lost me. Most of that psychology stuff is too deep for me. You must have had a lot of it."

"Three semesters. I quit school after my sophomore year."

"What for?"

"So I could be a cop, of course."

Phil snorted politely. "And I suppose you've never regretted it?"

His tactless questions irritated me slightly, like dirt under my fingernails, but I was too tired to evade them. "Sure, I've regretted it. I've had nine years to regret it. I was just a kid then. I wanted excitement. Instead of riding out the dull spots like most kids I quit, and picked up my badge. Christ, look around you, Phil. For headquarters, we've got the oldest public building in this town. The floors are buckled. The walls are grimy. The lighting is bad. The whole place smells like a waterfront mission. There aren't enough fans to go around so in summer the heat bakes the juice out of us. And the man I work for doesn't make things any nicer." I decided I was talking too much and put a cigarette into my mouth, then removed it and dropped it in the wastebasket. My hands were restless. "That's enough bitch session for one evening," I said. "Let's get back to work."

Phil thumbed aimlessly through the account books. "I don't suppose there was much chance Smithell was being blackmailed," he said.

"Look what happened to Veilleux."

"Yeah." Phil slid off the desk and went to the window. It had become perceptibly lighter outside as dawn neared. The air was cooler and the bug swarms around the light globes had thinned. For me the best part of the day was coming, early morning with sunlight a pale wash on the faces of the buildings, coming through the high windows to slant orange against the dirty walls. For me dawn was the dispatcher nodding sleepily as the speaker issued a broken crackle of static, the long walk past the cleared benches and down swabbed halls, the cup of coffee next door and the feel of stubble on my chin. It was the time for forgetting, for pushing back into a far place of mind the long dreary hours and the shambling people, and the hopelessness they wore along with their shoddy clothes.

Phil picked up the phone and dialed. He put one foot on the radiator and rested one elbow on the butt of the revolver he wore on his belt.

"Russ? What are you guys doing? You haven't found anything yet?" A pause. Then Phil looked at me, curled a hand over the mouthpiece. "No sign of any money anywhere else in the house."

"Call 'em off. They've been out there two hours."

"Okay," Phil said. "You guys come in. Lock up tight." He hooked the receiver.

"Well, what the hell did Smithell do with the money?" he said.

He was looking at me, not hopefully, but with a tired grouchy expression as if he had been asking questions like that forever and no one had ever bothered to answer. This time I had an answer. I could have forgotten then what I had learned in the past two hours, what must be true. The rest of the money would never be accounted for, and we would be subject to the fishy eye of the Federal men for a couple of days before they departed. Maybe we wouldn't find the money anyway. It would make things a lot easier, if I just forgot. After nine years as a cop and far too many compromises with myself I didn't shine very brightly any more, but if I tried to ignore the reasons that the money was gone there would be nothing left of me at all. I knew. As I looked at Phil to tell him I felt a small warning that I had never really known trouble before compared to what was going to come and, in a way, I was glad of it.

"I don't think he did anything with it," I said. "Someone stole it."

Phil looked strangely at me. "You think Jimmy Herne knew about the money?"

"Maybe. If he knew about it, sooner or later maybe he'd make up his mind to steal it. Thinking about all that cash in the basement could wear away his resistance."

Phil cleaned wax out of one ear with his little finger. "But why would he bother with those other trinkets—the watch and the cuff links, the small change from Smithell's wallet—when he had that much money in his hands? And would he have to kill Smithell to get into the storage room?"

"That's what I mean."

Phil came back to my desk. "He could have broken in, or got the key some night when Smithell was asleep, and blown town with the suitcase. With a few hours' head start he could have been halfway to Mexico before Smithell woke up." His eyes were troubled.

"Sure. But if I knew Smithell," I said, "and I knew about the money in the basement, I'd wonder about it, wonder why it was there. I might decide he came by it illegally. In which case, some of it might as well be mine. If I underestimated Smithell, as a lot of people did, I'd put it up to him, not knowing he can react in a nasty way under such circumstances. To my surprise I might be forced to defend myself and hit him too hard, so that he died. So the money would be mine by default but now I would have another problem—murder. Knowing all about Jimmy Herne I would take Smithell's watch and pocket money and other things and set the kid up for a frame. Then I would grab the money and leave. I'd realize there would be a good chance Jimmy would run like hell when he found Smithell's body. Even if he stuck it out Jimmy would have a tough time with the cops. In time he might even be persuaded to confess to something he never did at all."

I watched Phil, to see how he would receive it. I thought I knew him as well as anybody could. Long ago he must have accepted with a kind of bewilderment the savage world which didn't want him or his law and had gradually evolved into a cop who worked hard and competently, for no good reason. Like others, he felt pity sometimes, and anger sometimes, but always with some detachment. His face got dirty and sweat trickled down his back and his feet ached, as with other cops, and he felt irritation with his job now and then and dreamed of the ten days off each year and casually despised most politicians. He had found the pace that was suitable to him and had followed it. He wasn't a do-gooder, or a trouble-maker, or a tough guy. He wasn't particularly ambitious. We got along with each other, without affection, neither of us finding anything of interest in the other. We got along, and I thought I knew the book on him.

But now there was something in his eye, a coldness, a forming anger he probably wasn't even aware of yet. Maybe he never would be. But it was an indication, something on which to base the dissatisfaction I had noticed in him lately. There was something changing in him and maybe it was at the worst possible time, so close to retirement.

"You don't think Jimmy killed Smithell?" he said cautiously, knowing the way the trouble would breed, because it had been seeded deep and long ago. But there remained that something in his eye, that cold slow anger, as if he could see Jimmy Herne lying dead in the jail.

I said, "Jimmy never killed anybody. He's not even responsible for his own death."

He took out a cigarette and lit it. There was a tremor in his hands that he stilled. He screwed his face tight around the cigarette, puffing quickly.

"What do we do now, Bill?"

"We'll have to tell Gulliver."

"He went home half an hour ago. Are you going to wake him up to tell him?"

"I guess not. In the morning, after I get some sleep. I'll be able to think better."

The tremor he had quieted seemed to have spread inside him, so that he sat with a look of effort on his face. It seemed as if there still remained something to be said, and we both knew it.

"You want me to go with you?" he muttered.

"You want to go?"

He didn't answer me. He didn't look at me.

"It's my responsibility," I said heavily. "I'll tell him."

"Your responsibility," Phil said derisively, dropping the

cigarette on the floor and crushing it with his foot.

"He was only doing what he thought was right. He thought Jimmy was guilty."

"Do you think you're going to change his mind?"

"I'll tell him what we found out. He can't overlook it."

Phil said bitterly, "Quit kidding yourself. You know what's going to happen."

"Go on home, Phil," I said wearily.

I heard him walk, alone, down the hall, stop at the water cooler, and drink.

I POUNDED ON THE SCREEN DOOR OF THE ROOMING HOUSE AT 62 Davis Street for two minutes before a skinny character wearing a pair of striped shorts and nothing else came loping down the stairs, scowling fiercely.

"Whadda hell you want?" he said. "We got people tryna sleep in here and you waken 'em up."

"I want to see Stella."

"You crazy? You know what time it is? It ain't even five o'clock yet!"

"I know what time it is." I used the badge, although I didn't want to. "Get her up."

"Aw," he muttered, "cop. Crappo." He unhooked the screen, yawning. "You waid down here an' I'll get her."

I waited just inside the hall. I could hear her coming down the stairs, rapidly at first, as if she were taking the steps two at a time, then slower. In the dim hallway she seemed like a shadow until her head moved slightly and clear gray light from the open door showered over the ruffled blonde hair and one cheek.

"Bill?" she said, and I didn't answer right away because I was having some funny trouble with my breathing. She walked closer to me, until I could see her face.

"Bill, did you change your mind about—"

I raised my hand and took hold of one arm gently. "No. I didn't come to arrest you."

I could have drawn her to me, then, but I waited just too long and she pulled away from my hand, turning her face away from the door. There was no expression in her eyes.

Inside me I felt a hard spot of hopeless anger. I thought, what's the use? I can't tell her about Jimmy. I don't know why it matters, because she's no damn good, but I can't tell her and watch her indifference harden into hate.

"I guess you got into trouble because of me," she said.

"We had some talk about it. I won my point."

"Thanks, Bill. Was there something else . . .?"

"We did a lot of checking last night. We found out that Smithell was a bank employee a few years back. He had another name then. He skipped out with about forty thousand bucks and eventually turned up in Cheyney. The man in the trunk tried for a long time to find Smithell. When he did, he was killed."

I couldn't get myself to go on and give her my theory about Jimmy having been framed.

But she was just tired enough to accept what she had heard without too much astonishment. Her lips curved slightly. "Funny, isn't it? Everyone thought it was so noble of him to take a chance with Jimmy. A poor kid whose greatest offense was pilfering. But Smithell was a bank robber and a murderer, you tell me—and everybody thought he was so wonderful." She looked at me soberly. "I have to go back to bed, Bill. I have to be at the cafe at seven."

This time I caught her and held her as close to me as her resisting body would allow.

"Some day," she said deliberately. "I'm going to make you understand about Jimmy. I'll prove he killed no one. I'll prove you cops killed him."

"Oh," I said. "So that's it."

She twisted violently away from me, hair flopping over her forehead. "Let me alone," she said in an ugly voice. "Go away."

"You won't let him die. You have to hate me, because you think I could have done something. But—"

She turned and walked away from me, toward the stairs, ducking her head slightly to one side as she pushed hair off her forehead.

I followed her. "Stella!"

She turned on the stairs and looked at me. I couldn't see her face well. I thought I saw contempt there. And I thought I saw something else.

I slammed the screen door on my way out. Hard.

Why did she have to feel sorry for me?

5

GULLIVER was in his office next morning when I came in with four hours' sleep, a fresh shave and an old bird's nest in my mouth that two cups of hot black coffee hadn't disturbed.

I knocked once on his door and was invited in. Gulliver was seated behind his desk and there was somebody in a chair facing him. Gulliver looked at me for about one second and lifted a finger, which meant I was to stay out of the way and keep my mouth shut.

He returned his attention to the person in the chair, giving him a patient stare that wasn't unfriendly but a hell of a long way from being kind. One of Gulliver's eyebrows was slightly raised, which meant he was out of sorts.

When the guy in the chair started to fidget, Gulliver said, in a gentle tone that made me look at him sharply, "Listen, Charley, we've had a lot of trouble with you, haven't we?"

Charley mumbled something apologetic.

"I've tried to give you every break," Gulliver went on. "I know how it is with you and the booze. Now, it doesn't make a bit of difference to me if you drink, just so you don't do it where we finally have to come along and pick you up because somebody complains. How many times have you been in this year? Three, isn't it?"

Charley nodded. He was a tall bony man with thick black hair, sideburns, and two days' beard. His face had the shapeless vein-burst look of a violent drinker. He wore a pair of old tennis shoes without socks, light blue denims smeared with tar that hadn't washed out. His sport shirt was yellow, with collar stitching in blue, and it looked new.

"Now what have I done for you, Charley?" Gulliver said.

"I gave you a chance to get out of that jail, to work out in the open for the city, cutting weeds or something, out in the fresh air where you could get a little sun and build up your strength instead of sitting around the jail all day gathering stink. I even put you on your honor that you'd work, and I didn't have somebody around all the time watching to see that you did. What do you do for me? You run off and you're gone for three days. It makes me look bad, Charley."

"I wanted to see my sister. I ain't seen my sister in two years," the man sniffed.

"Goddam," Gulliver said in exasperation. "It's all right with me if you want to see your sister. But it's not all right with me when you run off like that. I ought to give you another fourteen days. I don't know what the hell else to do with you."

"Aw," Charley said.

"What did your sister think about you?" Gulliver said.

The man lowered his head. "Aw, she wants me to come stay with her. She wants to get me off the booze. She says I ought to talk with the preacher there."

Gulliver rubbed his jaw. "Hot tiddy," he said bleakly. Then he said, "I don't know if you're too late for religion or not, Charley. All I know is I don't want to smell you drunk in my town again. I'll make a little bargain with you. I'll send you back to the jail for the six days you got left. I won't give you no more time. But when you've served out your sentence this time I want you to get out of my town and stay out. You got that? Never set foot in my town again."

He got up from behind the desk and came around to the man. Charley stood up. He was about a head taller than Gulliver, looked fifty pounds lighter.

"Deal, Charley?" Gulliver said with a smile, holding out his hand.

Charley managed a nervous smile and took Gulliver's hand. Gulliver's face changed. With a powerful jerk he brought the man stumbling closer, face slack with surprise and fear. Gulliver's left hand was useless. He brought his left arm up and twisted his body, so that his elbow smashed across Charley's mouth, snapping his head back.

Charley sagged, still held by Gulliver's hard right hand. Gulliver released his grip and Charley collapsed to the floor, gagging, blood from his mouth and broken lips puddling the floor. He made a helpless noise, resting on his elbows and knees.

He ducked his head so he could finger his damaged mouth without upsetting his balance. Then he started to get up, slowly. Gulliver kicked him in the knee and Charley fell again, crawled into a corner near me and sat up, holding his fingers at his chin so blood wouldn't drip on his new shirt. His eyes were sullen.

"Wait till I tell you to get up, next time," Gulliver admonished. He walked over and kneeled beside Charley. "Your mouth is all bloody," he said, shaking his head solicitously. He grasped the man's new shirt and ripped it apart, buttons tearing from the cloth.

"Stop," Charley said weakly. "Stop tearing my new shirt."

Gulliver ripped it again, tearing a piece loose with which he dabbed at blood on the man's lips.

Unexpectedly, Charley began to cry. He stopped trying to brush Gulliver's hands away and just cried.

"My sister gave it to me," he said, looking at the torn shirt. He said it over and over, brokenly, crying harder every time.

Gulliver stood and tossed the blood-smeared piece of shirt into Charley's lap. "Get out of here," he said without interest. "Go wait on the bench outside until somebody comes to take you over to the jail."

Clenching the piece of shirt in his fist, Charley got up awkwardly, using the wall at his back for support, rubbing at his eyes with his knuckles. There were blood trickles on his chin and his lips were already swelling badly. His hairy round belly showed through the gap in his shirt. He lurched toward the door and got his hand on the knob. He turned with hate in his eyes and looked at Gulliver.

"You dirty ————," he said. "You dirty ————."

Gulliver laughed.

The man edged the door open and went outside.

Gulliver turned to his desk and took a cigar. He peeled

away the celophane and looked at me. He seemed vaguely pleased.

Something in my face made half his mouth tilt in a puzzled smile. "You don't like it, do you?" he said.

"No. I don't like it."

He shrugged. "Well, what did you want me to do? Hold hands with him?"

Gulliver looked moodily at me. He turned and went to the window, adjusted the blinds so he could see out. Gulliver's office has air-conditioning, paid for by himself. He got the cigar going, came back to his desk. He was looking at the bad hand.

"I've been trying for so damn many years," he said, "to make you see that there is only one way to handle guys like that. You got to show them right off that they can't get away with a damn thing and if they try they get their nuts nailed to the deck."

He looked up, his face grim. He held the hand up to me, the wrist stiff, last two fingers permanently fixed.

"Look, Bill! Look at it! How would you like to have something like this? I'm telling you, Bill, you can't give them a break, not one lousy break, because if you do they'll step on your face and laugh. You've got to be twice as tough as they are or you can't survive."

His good fist pounded the desk. "Bill, I'm telling you, I'm trying to tell you, what I know, what I've learned from experience. I'm trying to explain that you can be only one kind of cop and still keep your sanity. You're . . . we're garbage men, Bill, but the garbage is human and we're up to our armpits in it every day."

He put the cigar in his mouth and talked around it. "Now, Charley there doesn't like me very much. But he'll remember a lot better what I said to him. You can't go around beating up on all the punks, of course. You got to know who's ripe for it, who'll remember a good punch in the guts the longest. It's psychology."

"Sure," I said, without inflection.

Gulliver put the cigar in an ashtray and sucked at his teeth. "I'm going down to the lake for fishing this afternoon," he

said. "I want to get through around here. You got anything
new on this Veilleux killing?"

"He was a guard at the same bank where Smithell worked,"
I said. "Eight months after Smithell disappeared Veilleux
quit his job. Nothing on him after that time. He probably had
a lead nobody else picked up and was trailing Smithell. When
he found him he tried to cut himself in on the bank money
and got knifed for his efforts."

"That's the way I had it figured," Gulliver said. "Where's
the rest of the money?"

"I don't know. I think I know what happened to it, but I
don't know where it is."

I explained carefully what I had found out, telling him the
same things I had told Phil. He listened contemplatively, in a
haze of cigar smoke, hardly moving at all, his eyes fixed on
the tip of the cigar in his right hand.

"Well," he said, "that's pretty good, Bill. Good job of
thinking. Trouble is, it won't wash." He gave me the cheery
eye, but his mouth was turned down at the corners. "Jimmy
shot it full of holes by confessing."

"Goddamn it," I said, "how many times do I have to explain? Jimmy didn't kill Smithell. I just spent five minutes
telling you—"

Gulliver's mad eyebrow jerked up sharply. "That kid said
he killed Smithell. He told us how and why and what he did
with the stuff he took and I got it all down in writing and he
signed it. Here. You want to read it again? You want to re-
fresh your memory—?" He tugged at a desk drawer.

"What's the matter with you?" I said. "You can't even make
yourself believe it any more. You spent three days, five hours
at a crack, working that kid over until his tongue was so
thick he couldn't say his own name and finally he signed that
piece of fiction and now you think you've got a closed case.
It wouldn't be closed if Jimmy hadn't gone off the deep end
with his shirt around his neck. And it's not going to be
closed any more. We can't help that poor little bastard but
maybe we can help ourselves if we go back and pick up a
cold trail and try to find the right—"

"Get out," Gulliver said. He was trying to flex that wrist, and not doing very well at all.

"No. You're going to listen—"

He lunged half out of the chair, was stopped by the desk. "Get out! I said it was closed. He did it. He said he did it, and I got it right here, to show you. What do you want, you want my job, you want to make me look bad so you can get my job? I been watching you. I could tell, you think you're so goddam smart, figuring it all out, but you can't make a lie out of what he said, he signed it, you're not going to make me look bad!"

"You—if you'd—"

He put his hands on the edge of the desk, his face reddening, bulging with strain, cords thick in his neck. He heaved, and the desk toppled over.

"I told you to get out! Get out of here before I kill you!" He raised the damaged left hand. "It was two of them, in an alley, two like that Herne kid, and I was supposed to take it easy with them too, I guess, even when they did this to me. Oh, everybody was very sorry, but I just couldn't stay with the department any more, because everybody knows a cop has to have two good hands and I was a damned cripple because those kids—"

"All right," I said. "All right."

He fell back into the chair. "Get out and don't come back. You're through. You're suspended until you've had time to think it over and remember who you are working for around here. Get out before I break your lousy neck!"

"All right," I said. My mouth was dry. I went to the door and tried to open it, my hand slippery on the knob. The knob wouldn't turn correctly for some reason and my guts were tight as I waited for him to come after me. I could hear him breathing. That was all. I got the knob turned and went outside and shut the door quickly. I leaned against the wall and felt perspiration slide down my face.

Ramsey, the desk man, looked over his shoulder at me. "Something wrong in there?" he said.

"No," I said. "Not really." There was a sick taste in my

mouth. "Things just sort of blew apart. Nothing's really wrong, that I can't fix. Just watch me. I'll fix everything."

"Yes, sir," he said, cocking a worried eye at me.

I WAS DRUNK, DRUNK, DRUNK.

It was hot in the cell, my apartment.

There was the whiskey bottle, in my hand, and I had another drink and was happy to lie on the rug with sweat in my eyes. I didn't have any clothes on.

I had to shut all the windows and pull the blinds so he couldn't get in. But he got in anyway. He was there. In the mirror on the wall. I saw him sometimes, when I got up. Me. A looney. Boy oh boy. He was one. With hair in his face and that mask. Actually, I suppose, it wasn't a mask. Just that little scar under his eyes and his eyebrows which made it look like. Looney, though. He kept talking to me, serious. I tell you. He made me feel nervous. He made all the memories come back.

What happened, he said. What happened to the boy who was going to be such a great lawyer? What is he doing now? Is he studying law?

How should I know? I said.

I'll tell you what he's doing, he said. He's a cop. How tragic.

Like Gulliver, I said. I looked over my shoulder. I felt nervous again. I took another drink. He had a bottle, too. I looked at him when he didn't know it. The looney with hair in his eyes. He was drinking, too. I felt sorry for him. Like I wanted to cry. So sorry.

Gulliver stole him, I said.

The looney, the one in the mirror, nodded. It's Gulliver's fault, he said.

Let's forget about Gulliver.

Let's talk about the great lawyer, he said. The one who's a cop.

No, I said. Get out of here. I threw the whiskey bottle at him. Almost empty, anyway. He went away with a big crash, and there was nothing. Just a wall.

I knew he'd be back. Somewhere else. But if I just stayed there, just sat there on the rug, I wouldn't have to see.

I giggled.

There was someone at the door.

Pounding.

"Umcomin'."

"Bill, open up!"

Hard to see. Sweat in my eyes. There. Ooops. Got to rest. Tired. Lean against the wall because everything's dizzy-dizzy. Say. Who let the light in?

"Bill!"

"What?" It's a woman. A dame. And you haven't got any clothes on.

"Come on, Bill."

"Where we goin'?"

"To sit on the couch. Before you fall down. How could you get so drunk?"

"Well—"

"Sit down."

"Hell with you. I got perfect command my—" Oh, well.

"My God, it's hot in here. You're dripping wet. What did you shut the windows for?"

Zip. The blinds. The light hurt my eyes. I shut them.

"Come," she said. She took my hand. She was strong. We walked a long way and she had to help me. She made me get on my knees. She held my head together and pushed it under the cold water. Then she pushed me into the water.

"Wash yourself off. You smell. Couldn't you find the bath?"

"Go away. I'm not real any more. I'm images in pieces of broken mirror. That's me and that's me and that's me but not really me because I never was."

"Bill!" She hit me across the face. I looked at her. I saw her. There was a look of ferocity in her set white face. "Goddam you, sober up! I need help, and you're the only one I can trust. Help me, you—"

"Lots coffee," I mumbled.

She sighed. "All right," she said.

When she was gone I floundered upright in the tub, faced the cold spray and shook helplessly, grinding my teeth. She came back with the coffee and I turned off the shower, stepped out dripping on the bath mat and drank a cup, hot and black. She threw a bath towel at me, went into the bedroom and brought my robe. I put it on. I drank another cup of coffee.

"God," I said.

"Better?" Karis said.

"I'm living."

"What brought this on?"

"Gulliver. Son-of-a-bitch. Jimmy Herne didn't kill Smithell. Gulliver wouldn't listen. I'm through. So he thinks. But I'll make him listen."

"Jimmy Herne didn't kill Smithell? Who did?"

"How should I know? Maybe I'll find out."

I reached for her with a lurching motion of arms, caught her, held her. "This is for hitting me," I said. I kissed her, feeling her lips soften, feeling her succumb to the warmth of the kiss. She pulled away and there was an intense look of nothing at all in her wide eyes.

"Will you help me?"

"With what?"

"I called and called you, all morning. I tried to get hold of you, tried everywhere. I didn't know you were—"

"Damn it, what's wrong?"

"Nathan. He didn't come home last night. I can't locate him. He must be in trouble!"

"What do you want me to do?"

She was close to tears. "Find him. Find him!"

I shook my head. "If you don't know where to look, how—"

Her lips pressed together. "Bill—please—"

I sat on the edge of the tub. "Stop that. Did you try all the booze joints?"

She nodded.

"He may be shacked up somewhere. I don't know." I thought for a few seconds, then went into the bedroom and started pulling on my clothes. When I was dressed I went into the living room. Karis was on the sofa.

"Nathan shouldn't be too hard to trace," I said, "if he started off with a round of the bars and then got picked up, somebody will have seen him. What time is it?"

She looked at her watch. "Ten after four." I set mine.

"I'm going out for a little while," I said. "I won't be long. You can wait here if you want to."

IT WAS LATE SUNDAY MORNING AND THERE WERE ONLY A few cars parked in the courtyard of Roxy Marko's place. The bar was closed. I went up the stairs to Roxy's office.

With my duplicate key I opened the door about an inch, exercising great caution, and immediately heard voices. One was Roxy's, a different voice from what I knew. His tone was contemptuous, caustic, designed to make the one he was talking to feel a vast inconsequentiality.

"Doctor, I could ruin you overnight."

The other voice was deeper, a church-choir bass. "You can't ruin a man already ruined."

Roxy laughed delightedly. "Doctor, what's got into you? For a ruined man, you've got the best practice in the city." His voice was shaded with sudden knowledge. "Oh, I see what you mean, Dr. Einhorn. You've developed a conscience. A bad thing for a man of medicine. All doctors should be born without it. Why don't you have it removed surgically, doctor?"

"I hate your damned guts," the doctor said distinctly.

Roxy laughed again. "Well, doctor. Am I fond of you? No. But once you liked me well enough. When the girl died."

"I can't be blamed for that. You knew what she had tried to do before you sent her to me. She was dying already. I didn't know, not until I saw the mess in her uterus."

"But you can be blamed for not reporting her death," Roxy said softly. There was a repetitive sound, as if his heel was hitting the side panel of his desk.

The doctor's voice was a dirge. "I needed the money. You knew I needed the money. I wish I had given it back."

I looked over my shoulder, saw no one in the foyer below. I didn't move.

Roxy's voice lashed. "When did you start wishing that? The same time you started thinking about stealing the bottle?"

"I never should have given it to you in the first place!"

"And if you could steal it back?"

"I'd throw it away. Destroy it. Why do you want it? What good is it going to do you?"

"What good did it do me when that girl died in your office, doctor?"

"She wasn't important. She was just a—"

"Tramp? What a noble attitude."

"I'm sick," the doctor whimpered. "I've been so sick because of it. One mistake. Just one."

"How long have you been brooding like this, doctor? It's not good for you. You might take to drink."

"Look, you can quit toying with me. You can put your gun away. I'm not going to do anything foolish."

"No, you've been foolish enough for one day. But I won't put the gun away yet. I like to point it at you, doctor. I like to see the look on your face. I want to see what happens when I do this."

A hammer was cocked.

"Oh," Roxy said gleefully. "You should see yourself, doctor. You really look like you need a drink. But I forgot. You're not a drinking man." There was a sound, of metal striking lightly on glass. "This little cocktail is made to order for you, doctor. Your first drink and your last."

A drawer slid open. "I'm putting the bottle here, doctor," Roxy said. "It's never locked. The bottle will be here. If it isn't here some time, I'll know who took it."

"May I go?"

"I want you to forget this, doctor," Roxy said. "I want you to forget the girl and what you've tried to do today. I don't want you to think about it. It's not good for you. It's not good for your soul." Roxy chuckled. "Your soul. Tell me about your soul, doctor. Everybody is supposed to have one. Is it round or kidney-shaped? Is it alabaster, or black with sin? Where is it? Behind the liver? In your scrotum? That would be the place for mine, if I had one."

"I'm quite sure you don't," the doctor said.

"Get out of here, doctor," Roxy said wearily.

I locked the door, retreated down the thickly carpeted

steps three at a time. I was standing in front of the bar entrance frowning at the *closed* sign when Dr. Einhorn came down the stairs, slowly. I could see his reflection in the glass squares of the door. He was a medium-tall man wearing a light gray suit and string tie. He walked with a sort of labored dignity, as if he were being taunted by street urchins and couldn't quite ignore them. There were dim reflections of hell in his sad eyes.

Thirty seconds after he had driven away I went up the stairs again and knocked on Roxy's door.

"Yes?"

"It's Bill."

"Oh. Come on in." He opened the door.

In his office, Roxy took a stand in front of the two windows that afforded a view of the courtyard. There was a trace of sunlight on his face. He sniffed once, and freckles jiggled on his nose. He turned and looked at me, his face serene. But he seemed tired, drained of energy and emotion. The mouse had died, and it wasn't fun to pull his tail any more.

"You look rough," he said. "Who dug at you?"

"I never could handle my women," I said stiffly.

"Liquor either," Roxy said critically. He sat down behind the desk, picked up a .32 revolver, the hammer cocked. He punched the cylinder from the frame, took out one of the cartridges, clicked the cylinder into place and pulled the trigger. He put the gun in a drawer.

"Social call?" he asked.

"Nah. A little private business. I'm looking for Nathan Fisher."

A tiny crease appeared between Roxy's eyes. "He's missing?"

"His sister says he hasn't been home all night. She knows him well enough to think he might be tied up with a dame somewhere. He throws a shoe every now and then."

Roxy nodded, the frown deepening. He picked up the brass cartridge, held it meditatively with two fingers. "I know the boy. I think a lot of him."

"He told me once that he knew you. His sister is worried sick. A bad press would finish him in this state."

. "Don't I know it," Roxy said, almost worriedly. "I told him to stay out of trouble." He glanced at me for enlightenment. "What is it with the talented kids like him? They've got all the chance in the world and they can't stay off liquor."

"He's got troubles of some kind. He can't forget his wife."

Roxy nodded, put out a hand to his phone. "If he'd been to any of my places I'd know about it." He let the hand rest indecisively on the desk.

"You been backing him?" I said.

"Some. I think he has promise." A swift intuitive gleam in his eye. *There are other mice.* "Do you want me to see if I can find him?"

"That's why I came to you. You can do it ten times faster than me. I think it's important to track him quick."

Roxy shook his head, as if he doubted his ability. "I'll see what I can do. If I find out where he is, will you put him to bed?"

"Sure."

"Maybe you ought to give him a good spanking first," Roxy said disgustedly. "Where can I reach you, Bill? It might take a while."

"My place."

He drew his little finger across the small mustache on his lip and reached for the phone, his eyes fixed with thought.

I WENT HOME. KARIS HAD CLEARED UP MOST OF THE MESS I had made. I told her Roxy was looking. She mentioned that she had heard of Roxy from Nathan. I explained that Roxy's connections were better than mine and that he would call me.

"I hope we don't have to wait long," she said without conviction. She toyed with a black heart-shaped button on her dress. It was a white dress, imprinted with large playing cards, the royalty of the deck depicted in caricature. She went into the bath to comb her crisp dark hair.

In the kitchen I made myself a light drink, took one sip and poured the rest in the sink. I settled down on the sofa with a bottle of ale, which I didn't really want either, and thought about Roxy. I had clues to him, through association, through others familiar with him. He was a good friend to many. He hated only those who dismissed him as insignificant because of his size and boyish look. His hatred could be deadly. Maybe it was the great motivating force in his personality. His strength was based on the weaknesses of others. I was his friend. I knew him only to be wary of him.

Roxy tended bar for Old Man Cluney down around the railroad yards once, before the flush years, before I came to Cheyney. I knew, from a good source, that he hadn't changed much since those days. He was quiet, and minded his own business, and had the smile for everyone, the wide dimpled smile that said nothing.

There was a fight in the place one night. Old Man Cluney was the throw-'em-out-on-their-cans roughhouse type. He was grappling with one of the drunks, and Roxy had a billy. Apparently, he hit the wrong man. It's easy to make that kind of mistake in a brawl. Anyway, Roxy admitted nothing and there were no witnesses. Old Man Cluney died, raving, three days later, with the back of his skull shattered. Roxy bought the place cheap from the widow. Roxy was lucky at poker, too.

Karis came out of the bath and sat down beside me. "You've got some explaining to do," she told me. "You said Jimmy Herne didn't kill Smithell. You said Gulliver wouldn't listen to you."

I nodded bitterly. "You might as well know the whole story." I explained briefly about Leland Smithell and the money and about Jimmy Herne. I didn't try to make myself look any better or worse than I was. I didn't mention Stella.

Karis had a hard time believing it at first. She talked about Smithell for a time, about the many evenings she and Nathan had spent at his house. She seemed dismayed that he had fooled people so completely. She decided that she couldn't dislike him as much as she should. "He was—well—sweet. A little gruff, maybe, but kind to everyone and sort of lonely." She put her hands over her face in resignation. "I'll never be able to see him as you do, Bill."

She tucked her long legs beneath her on the sofa. "I'm sorry, Bill," she said then. "I'm sorry for you."

That made two girls sorry for me.

"Because I made a mistake about Jimmy?"

"I don't think that was your fault. I'm sorry because you were suspended for trying to make Gulliver understand. Why can't he admit he was wrong?"

"I'm not enough of a psychologist to unravel that. Maybe to admit he could make so terrible a mistake would—well—destroy him. At least in his own eyes."

"What is he doing to you, Bill?"

"What do you mean?"

"Why did you get drunk?"

"I don't know. It was a crazy thing."

"Do you get drunk often?"

"Who can afford it?"

"That's what I mean. It was no ordinary drunk. Not with the windows closed and the shades pulled—you were frightened, I think. Are you afraid of Gulliver?"

"Miss Freud, I presume. Or is it Adler, or Jung?"

"All right. I'll stop analyzing. But it's only that I'm afraid too." Her nose crinkled as she grinned. Her brat grin. "What are you going to do, Bill?" she said in a lonely voice. "What are either of us going to do?"

"What are you afraid of?"

"That's the strange part. I don't know. These deaths next door—my brother, maybe—I just don't know!"

Looking at her, I remembered what a man named Eliot had said, about private terrors and particular shadows. Her hand clasped mine almost desperately, as if she were in danger of being carried away by her wild fleet thoughts.

"I realize you think I'm silly," she said. "But I tell you I'm scared. I'm scared and I can't help it. Oh, Bill," she wailed suddenly, "hold me. Please."

I held her, against my side, one arm across her shoulders, her head against my chest. I held her for a long time. Once, I lowered my head and kissed her on the tip of her ear. Her breasts moved under the dress as she slowly breathed. Her eyes were shut. Once she said:

"Do you think I'm beautiful, Bill?"

"I think you're really beautiful."

"So are you," she said. "Even that big, square head. Even that little scar."

The small scar on my puss had been left by a thug's bullet.

At five minutes of six the telephone rang alarmingly, and she sat up quickly, as if she had been awakened. The top of her head brushed my chin.

I went to the phone stand and picked up the receiver.

"Randall."

"This is Roxy." His voice sounded slightly hoarse. "I found him."

"Where?"

"Melverne."

"Any trouble?"

"Probably. He's in a bawdyhouse called Oakdale Rooms. A cab driver picked him up about four this morning and delivered him to the door. He's been inside ever since."

I could sense Roxy's concern. "Is that so bad?"

"These houses in Melverne are no local operation. Some Kansas City boys, I hear. The names aren't important. Offhand I can think of three politicians, one with a seat in Washington, who've mortgaged their careers to Kansas City people because of one night in Melverne. Get him out of there, Bill," he said urgently.

"All by myself?"

"Well, Donny Arlene did the tracking for me. He works for me, now and then. He's good. He'll help you. He knows the place. You can pick Arlene up in the Melverne bus station."

"I'll be there about seven."

"Bill," Roxy said, "take it easy. Some real hard boys keep their eyes on these houses. And after you tuck Nathan in, come and see me." He hung up.

"Where is he?" Karis said.

I turned around.

"Melverne. I'm leaving right now."

I went into the bedroom and put my gun on. Karis was standing by the front door when I came out.

"You might as well go home," I said. "I'll bring Nathan to you when I pick him up."

"I'm going with you," she said.

"No, you're not. Things could get rough. It's no place for you."

"Don't argue. I said I'm going with you. He's my brother. Where in Melverne is he?"

"He's in . . . in a—"

"You don't need to tell me," she said. "I'm familiar with his habits. Come on. I want him home."

6

DONNY ARLENE was about my height, five-ten. But he had shoulders like a Buick with both doors open. His hair was black and he combed it straight back without a part. He had a Roman nose, a black bar of eyebrows, heavy prominent cheekbones, a narrow chin and a beautiful, almost lecherous, smile. He was wearing a tweed sport coat and soft gray slacks.

The bus station was practically empty. I found Arlene on a stool in the coffee shop. He tossed me a look that took in everything and gave away nothing, the smile fading but still hanging around.

"Hello, there," he said. To the waitress he said, "This is a good friend of mine, honey baby. What's the name again, good friend of mine?"

"Bill Randall."

"Give my good friend Bill Randall a hot cup of coffee, baby doll." He whirled with the stool, winked at her. "There's something in it for you."

"You can skip the coffee," I said. "We're in a rush."

Arlene snapped his fingers. His every movement was made with impeccable grace. "That's right. There was something we had to do, wasn't there?"

He unseated himself, tugged at his coat, flicked at a spot of lint on his slacks, which looked as soft as cleansing tissue.

"Give me a call, you beautiful one, you," he tossed over his shoulder at the bemused waitress. "Cheyney six four two oh."

She spelled it out with her lips. Arlene tugged at his sport coat again, walked toward the door, balancing delicately, like a good dancer, a better fighter. I fell in behind him without being told.

"What's the weather outside?" he said back at me. "Looked like rain when I came in."

"It still looks like rain. My car is the Oldsmobile across the street."

"The '53? Nice job. What does it do?"

"It runs. Now and then."

He started across the street. His quick hungry eyes spotted Karis in the front seat, and he paused.

"Hey," he said. "A doll. Yours?"

"His sister. Shift into low. She's not in the mood."

"I'll give her the sixty-second quickie line. Have my little ol' finger in the pie before she knows it, man. Or would I be beating your time?"

"You couldn't beat it with a canoe paddle. Let's go before it rains. I wouldn't want you to fade."

He gave me more teeth and danced over to the car. I mean it. He skipped across the street and introduced himself to the front seat, letting one hip ride Karis over slightly. She took on a bemused expression, too.

"Baby," he breathed, "how do you do? I be Donny Arlene. You be Karis . . . uh, Fisher. Donny glad to meet Karis."

"Down, boy," from Karis.

We all got the dazzling grin.

"Quick, dad, the blinders," Karis said, without expression.

"The lady understands me," Arlene chortled, a hand resting lightly on her thigh. Karis took the hand and tucked it firmly into his breast pocket. Donny laughed explosively and sat up straight.

"Enough with the junior prom stuff," I said. "Roxy said you were a hot article. When do you get lit?"

His smile vanished, leaving his lips in a grim line. "I weigh one ninety-four, in shape," he said. "And I'm always in shape. I can take any two men your size. Wanna bet?"

"You interest me," I said. "Come over some time and we'll throw pablum at each other. Is it okay if now we stick to business?"

He shrugged. "The house is in a neighborhood a block

south of Highway 29. Old-time residential street. Most of the houses are stone crypts, built maybe fifty years ago." He glanced at Karis. "Does the lady know about . . . ?"

Karis nodded. "Go on."

"He's in one called the Oakdale Rooms," Donny continued. "There are two other something-or-other 'rooms' on the same street. Same set-up. An alley runs behind the place. The house is three stories, and a basement."

"Ever been inside?" I asked.

His eyes sidled in Karis' direction, but she was looking straight ahead. "A couple of times. Out of my income bracket, usually."

"What about the rest of the block?"

"Converted residences, mostly. An interior-decorating shop and some dentists' offices. There's a drug store on one corner. A couple of old Melverne families still live on the street. Won't give up their homes. The whole think is discreet. You wouldn't know what goes on unless you\were wised."

"How do we get there?"

Donny gave directions and I pulled out. We drove silently for a while through downtown Melverne. It was almost dark, partly because of the welts of storm clouds low in the sky.

Arlene said, "You heeled?"

"Forty-five revolver."

His eyes rolled. "Leave it on your belt. Even if you are a cop. We need any work like that, we use this." His hand came out of his coat pocket. It was holding a switch-knife. His thumb caressed the handle and the long thin blade jumped out, two inches above Karis' lap. She started nervously. Donny chuckled softly and put it away.

When we reached the right street I parked in front of the drug store. In a church nearby the congregation sang unevenly, above the low threatening sound of thunder.

"How do we work it?" I said. "You sure he's still inside?"

"I'm sure," Arlene said, patting his cheek lightly. He took out a package of gum, showed it around, took a stick for himself. "Getting in is easy. After that we just see how far we can push a bluff. You got your tin plate with you?"

I nodded.

Arlene went on, "I don't think it'll impress anybody much, but you never know." He touched the clipped edges of Karis' hair with a finger. His breath was on her cheek. "This doll here complicates things. I hadn't counted her in. She can't stay in the car. An unescorted dame can't sit in this neighborhood five minutes without getting picked up by the cops. They keep the streets swept clean. Shows you how well organized this burg is. On second thought, she might come in handy. What time is it?"

"Seven twenty-two."

Arlene put his narrow chin on his chest. He was thinking out loud. "It shouldn't take us longer than twenty minutes to get Fisher out." He took Karis' hand in his own and looked at her searchingly. "Honey baby, will you do what ol' Donny says? I want you to go in the drug store and wait until seven forty-five. Then drive to the east end of the alley"—he pointed —"and wait until you see three flashes." He opened the glove compartment and felt around for my flashlight. "From this. Then come batting down the alley and pick us up. Will you do that for Donny, honey?"

"Okay," Karis said dryly. She was beginning to get scared.

Donny patted her knee. "Good girl. Maybe when Donny brings your brother to you, you'll show Donny how much you appreciate—"

"Come on, lover," I said. "She'll think your feet are cold."

He gave me a smooth look of dislike, and the smile came and went like lightning flashing. I handed Karis the keys. She put a hand on my sleeve. "Bill—"

"I'll take good care of him, honey," Donny said. "Don't you fret about it."

Donny and I walked down the street toward the Oakdale Rooms. I could see the sign on a post near the sidewalk. *Reasonable*, it said. *Rooms*. I could smell the stale fruitiness of the gum Arlene was chewing. He hummed softly. "What a chick," he said once.

We went up the short walk to the small front porch. There was another sign, hand-lettered, beside the door. *No military personnel, please*, it advised.

"These people cater to the best," Arlene said. "There

are cribs over on the other side of town for the five-buck trade."

He rang the bell and we waited, standing around with the air of innocent expectancy it seemed proper to assume.

A small, delicate-waisted Chinese girl in a light blue maid's uniform opened the door.

"Please, come in," she said.

We marched into the foyer. There was a cheerful carpet covering the floor. The walls were painted light green and showed a few pictures, Audubon prints and the like. A radio played softly.

She took us to some kind of waiting room, with curtained doorways at each end. It was very still, and there was a faintly salty smell. This room was a little more spicy, with pictures of almost-undressed girls on the carnelian walls, each pose calculated to make a man think hard about what was up-stairs, without spoiling the surprise. Red is supposed to be a sensuous color, too.

Magazines were lying around on end tables, featuring nearly nude studies. The girls themselves, I knew, when they entered after an appropriate time lapse, would wear tight-fitting pajamas, slashed here and there to show a bare leg and hip and navel, or diaphanous gowns which obscured all but hid nothing. If you weren't in heat after this and the wash job upstairs, they called the undertaker.

"You wait," the little Chinese said. "Go bring girls. Have drink, if you wish."

"Where's Mother Garrett?" Donny said.

The Chinese hesitated perceptibly. Her eyes were mute. "Not here. I go bring girls." She turned toward the curtains at the far end of the room.

"Wait a minute," Donny said, tight-lipped, "and knock off that goddam pigeon talk. We want to talk to you."

She stopped but didn't turn. "What the hell do you want, buster?"

Arlene nodded at me, and I took out my badge. The girl moved her head enough to get one large shiny eye on it.

"A hackie brought a guy in here about four this morning," Arlene said. "He's still here. We want him."

She seemed to sigh a little. "You small-town clowns should know better than to try a pitch like this. Beat it while you still got your skins." She took two firm steps toward the curtains.

Arlene's eyes were narrow gashes, but the grin showed, evilly. "We can do it the hard way."

She gave him a small scornful smile and kept walking. Arlene moved slickly, without sound. He grasped her from behind, lifted her from the floor as if she were a large doll. He had a hand over her mouth. The other hand worked on her. She writhed, jerked suddenly, and a hard sick sound got past Arlene's broad hand. She jerked again, and stopped kicking.

"You going to behave?" he said in her ear.

She nodded.

He put her on the floor, held one of her wrists. Half her forearm was lost in his grip.

"Where's Fisher?"

"Yvonne's room."

"Take us."

"Think you're tough?" she gasped. "Think you're tough? Goddam sonuvabitching . . ."

"And keep those Frisco accents soft or—"

"Oahu," she snorted contemptuously, pulling her arm free and turning. "I was born in . . ."

He swung the edge of his palm against the back of her neck, just below the hanging shiny black hair, and she slipped quietly to the floor.

"Too much noise," Arlene said.

He picked her up quickly and draped her over one shoulder without effort. He went through the curtains and I followed. We were in a paneled hallway, with a wide flight of stairs on the left and three doors to the right.

"One straight ahead is the kitchen," he grunted. He picked out one of the other doors and opened it. "Think this is the basement. Good." He ducked his shoulder and the Chinese girl rolled off. I heard her flop down the steps, in the darkness. Arlene shut the door.

"Upstairs," he said. He had a comb in his hand, and he ran it through his hair several times. He tugged at his coat.

A blonde girl with an unbelievable bosom came around the

bend in the stairs. She was in pajamas. The pajamas were trying, anyway.

She blinked at us. "Looking for someone?" There was a big space between her front teeth.

Arlene said, "Where is Yvonne's pad?"

"Upstairs, to the left, two doors down. I think she's entertaining."

We squeezed past her. Arlene gave her stuck-out backside a slap, and she giggled mechanically.

We counted our way to Yvonne's room and knocked quietly. Somewhere in the house the strings of a guitar were being thoughtfully explored.

"Busy," we heard, through the door.

We went in anyway. It was a small neat room, with lavatory separate, and a closet door across from that. A double bed took up much of the space. Yvonne sat in an easy chair near the bed—another creamy blonde like the one on the stairs—reading. She was naked, except for a pair of socks on her feet. Nathan was sprawled face down on the rumpled bed. He was dressed the same as the girl, except he wasn't wearing socks.

She looked up from the book, not too surprised. Maybe she was in demand. "I said I was busy, boys."

"He's the one we want," Arlene said. I shut the door. The girl turned the book face down in her lap and looked at us. Arlene grasped Nathan by the shoulders, tried to sit him up. Nathan's mouth hung open, but his eyes stayed shut. He reeked. There was a nearly empty fifth of whiskey on a small table next to the bed.

Arlene let him drop. "What the hell did you do that with?" he asked he girl.

She got up languidly, went to the bed, looked at Nathan and laughed. "I separate the men from the boys."

"How much has he had to drink?" I said.

"Lots. He was drunk when he came. I worked the first load out of him, but he about killed my bottle a while back. He'll be dead for hours. Mother Garrett isn't going to like me talking to you."

"This for her," Arlene said, gesturing. "Where is she?"

"At church, I suppose. She always goes to the 7:15 service on Sunday night." She closed her eyes wearily. "Jesus, I'm bored."

Arlene grunted and began picking up Nathan's clothes from the floor. The girl looked at me as if she wanted conversation.

"He was restless all night," she said. "I didn't seem to help him any. He kept threshing around in his sleep and talking about somebody named Kelly. He asked Kelly to forgive him. I caught that much. There's something inside him that's trying to come out." She looked at me as if I could explain.

I shook my head once. A ventilating louver beside the closet door caught my eye. I went over and looked at it. I opened the closet door.

"Oh, Nathan, boy, please try to cooperate a little," Donny said as he wrestled with the limp Fisher, trying to dress him.

"I'd help you," the girl said, "but like I said, Mother Garrett won't like it."

I went into the closet and stood on tiptoe to look through the louvered vent. It afforded a good view of the bed. I ran my fingers around the rear wall of the closet, found a sliding panel. This led into another closet in the next room. I went back into the room Nathan occupied.

Arlene had Nathan's shirt on him, partly buttoned. He held Nathan in a sitting position on the edge of the bed with one hand. With the other he forced Nathan's right foot into a shoe.

The girl was looking at me and yawning. "Why so unhappy?" she said.

"Who's been taking pictures?"

She looked blankly at me. "Pictures?"

"Through the air vent," I said. "Don't give me a stall. I know what the side take on home movies is in a pad like this one." I unbottoned my coat and pushed it back far enough so she could see the butt of the .45.

"Say," she said. "Say."

"Is there a darkroom in the house?"

"Mother Garrett," she began weakly, not taking her eyes from the gun. "Mother Garrett won't . . ."

"You're not saying the right words." I looked at my watch. We had been inside fourteen minutes. "Come on, where is it?" I reached down and pulled her from the chair by the arm. "I . . . I can't . . . I . . ."

I began to twist the arm. She bent almost double, raising one foot off the floor. "Oh . . . you hurt . . . oh . . ."

"Where is it?"

"In . . . in the basement—don't—don't . . ."

"Was somebody taking pictures today?"

"Yes, yes. God . . ."

"You know who your guest is?"

"No. And I don't care."

"Sit down." I thrust her toward the chair.

"But don't get comfortable," Arlene said. He had finished dressing Nathan. "Put on a robe or something and show me out of here. The back way."

"I'm going after the darkroom," I said. "I'll join you later."

"Okay, but snap it up. That maid won't stay cold forever." He gave me the big grin. With the scent of the place in his nostrils, he was nervous as a satyr.

I left the room as Donny was shouldering Nathan. Melancholy chords from the guitar still sounded from somewhere. I raced down the steps without encountering anyone.

There was a small landing at the top of the basement stairs. I carry around a small flashlight, about the size and weight of a fountain pen. I took it out and started down the steps into the solid blackness of the basement.

I flashed the light around as much as I dared but didn't see the Chinese girl. I couldn't take time to worry about her.

The stairs divided near the basement floor, forming a rough T with the main flight, and there was a small deck with a railing at the juncture of the steps. I stood there for a few slow seconds, trying to adjust to the darkness.

Finally I exposed the beam of the flashlight and let it drift across the stained concrete floor, over packing crates, old furniture, cold furnace. A pair of oblique yellow eyes gleamed at me as a sleek brown cat near the furnace looked up from a saucer of sardines.

In one corner of the basement I saw a small structure fashioned of two frame walls at right angles to the basement walls. In case I was wondering, a neat sign on the door of the little room said: *DARKROOM—keep out when door is shut.*

I found my way over to it, using the flashlight sparingly, and edged the door open. A small balding man was bent over a sink inside, swishing prints in a shallow pan, his skin and clothing blood red. I stepped inside, stumbling over a raised floor. He turned in the crimson gloom, a small fat devil with ferret eyes. He reached beneath his black rubber apron. I jammed him against one wall as he pulled his knife, and it jarred from his fingers. Neither of us uttered a sound. I hit him below the heart and he slid to the floor.

It was hot in the little room and I could smell myself. In a small dusty mirror over the sink my face glistened wetly, eyes slitted and secretive, mouth drawn tight in a fiery skull.

There were prints and negatives of nudes everywhere, stacked on the sink, pinned to a length of wire to dry. There were small rolls of movie film. I looked at nothing, just grabbed all photos which showed men and women in the close harmony of love and stuffed my pockets full. The photographer lay sprawled against the wall, head lolling on one shoulder. One eyelid hadn't completely closed.

He watched me.

The faucet dripped nervously.

Hurriedly I searched through the accumulation of pornography. When my pockets were full, I stuffed the pictures inside my shirt. I realized suddenly I couldn't take them all. There was a filing cabinet drawer full of prints and negatives. I didn't know which were recent. I stacked them together, ripped them, crumpled the pieces. Sweat rolled down my face. The drawer was empty, the floor littered. I shut the drawer.

I eased the stubborn door of the darkroom open, looked outside.

It was even blacker than I remembered.

I started toward the stairs. My shoes scuffled twice on the concrete floor. I walked slowly, afraid to use the flashlight. I remembered the red eye of the photographer, how he had watched me. Maybe he hadn't been unconscious. I could sense him walking behind me, stealthily. My breath panicked in my throat.

I was near the stairs. I had to use the flashlight now, so I wouldn't stumble over them. My thumb had trouble with the button.

I turned it on.

A white, disembodied face wavered above me. It was a man's face.

He blinked.

He looked down at me.

I stepped back, my body numb and chill from shock.

Lights jumped on all over the basement. The shock diminished slowly. Two men stood side by side on the deck near the basement floor. The taller one had a gun. He rested his weight on one forearm against the railing, and his revolver pointed negligently at the floor.

A woman stood at the bottom of the steps, her hand over a light switch on the railing. Her hair was white-blonde, neatly waved. She was a handsome woman, about forty-five, with shrewd dark eyes, and expertly made up to hide bad skin. She looked coldly at me.

The two men waited, disinterestedly alert. The taller man watched me steadily, as if wondering how I should be killed. He had already decided that I was going to be killed.

"Church over already?" was all I could say. I was scared spitless.

"See if he's got a gun, Rorry," she said.

The shorter man, who had a large bulky body on short narrow legs, flexed his fingers. It was as far as he got.

"Don't touch him, you bastards," Arlene said from the top of the stairs. All eyes went to him.

Donny crouched; his coat was stretched tightly over his muscled shoulders, his face a grimace of strain. The tall man brought the gun up swiftly, one hand gripping the railing tightly. I reached for my own gun. Donny was an absurdly easy target, and in the tight close seconds before death would erupt I wondered bleakly if he had lost his mind. Then I realized what he was doing.

They saw, too, just as the heavy icebox toppled and fell

toward them. The top hit one of the steps, and the icebox skidded crazily and turned sideways, rolled over and over down the stairs, making an unholy racket, all in the space of three quick heartbeats.

Both men gaped at the descending refrigerator a split second too long. They turned in panic and met each other. The taller one, who had quicker reflexes, jumped backward and toppled over the rail to the floor six feet below. The other tried to turn and claw his way over the railing. The tumbling mass of steel caught up with him and smashed him through the railing with a harsh ripping sound of old wood. He screamed thickly once, most of his body pressed to the floor beneath the weight of the refrigerator, his arms waving wildly as if he were trying to swim; then a gigantic convulsion left him limp and unconscious.

The other man still clutched his gun. He was crouched slightly with his arm outstretched, sighting Arlene. This boy knew what it was about. I threw back my coat, pulling the .45, knowing I didn't have time to do anything but empty the gun in his direction. Arlene was screaming frantically. I started shooting as the barrel nosed up. I got lucky with two of them. Through the haze of smoke I saw his forearm smashed somewhere near the elbow and his own revolver jumped and disappeared, as if he had said the magic word and committed it to limbo. In the same instant another slug caught him in the side and he jerked, walked forward two tipsy steps with his mouth open and fell forward to the steps, crying loudly.

My other slugs had ricocheted from the concrete walls with ear-splitting trills to punctuate the echoing blasts from the .45. I was lucky I didn't get one of my own slugs back, the size of a quarter after gouging the walls. My brain was slightly dizzy. It's no joke to empty a .45 in a closed room within three seconds. A little bit like walking too close to a speeding locomotive while somebody smacks the back of your head with a board.

When I sorted my thoughts after things had quieted down I saw Mother Garrett scrambling around in her purse. Arlene raced down the stairs, launching a kick that tore the purse from her grasp. He fell on top of her. She shrieked vilely and speared one of his eyes with a finger.

He crawled around and around on the floor, his eye squinted shut, cursing hysterically. She kicked for his weak spot, but the kick was weak and the pointed heel dug harmlessly into his stomach. He grabbed her shoe and wrenched it from her foot. He tucked his face against his chest so she couldn't get at it easy, clawed his way up her body and grabbed her by the blouse, tearing it and her brassiere completely from her body as she whirled and staggered to her feet. He followed, hit her in the jaw with his fist. She moaned, hurt, and her hands dropped. He held her by the hair with one hand, slapped her viciously, right and left. He let her drop. She kneeled on the floor, holding herself, her skirt pulled down around her thighs.

"Teach . . . you . . ." Arlene muttered, squirming his body aimlessly, his feet planted. He held a hand over his injured eye. His mouth was twisted in pain. Hair hung over his forehead.

He stumbled toward the wounded hood lying in pain against the stairs, kneeled beside him, found a blackjack in one of the man's pockets. He jerked the man's head up by the hair and, ignoring the man's quick plea, used the leather sap across his chin.

Arlene waved the sap in the air. "My eye, my eye! I ought to kill her."

I took hold of his shoulder.

"Okay, okay," he said. "Let's shag out of here, man."

We trotted up the stairs.

In the hallway the Chinese girl leaned against the phone stand, dialing with an unsteady finger. Arlene stopped long enough to hurl her out of the way, rip the phone from the wall.

He dove for the kitchen door, me following. We crossed the kitchen fast and he put his shoulder against the screen door opening on the back porch, banging it wide, and we leaped into the yard, ignoring the back steps. He ran toward the alley. I saw my car, the headlights bright moons in the darkness.

"Where's Nathan?" I yelled.

"In the heap. Move the feet, man!"

Two doors of the Oldsmobile were open. Arlene and I scrambled inside and Karis dug out, spraying gravel against the high board fence on the other side of the alley. Behind us, in the house, rose a tentative scream. Lights were on all over the place. I glanced back at Arlene. He was still holding a hand to his eye. Beside him, Nathan slept blissfully, his head rolling as Karis wrestled the wheel.

"Took care of one phone," Arlene panted. "Probably others."

My breath was scorching my throat. "Think they'll sic the cops on us?"

"No. Not worth while. Let's get some distance anyway, honey baby." He sucked in air. "Old bitch blinded me. I'm hurt. Really hurt."

"Let's see," I said. Karis swung left, screechingly, onto the highway, ignoring a yellow light. I took a swift look at her. Her lips were molded into a hard line. There was perspiration on her forehead. She seemed slightly stunned, but she was handling the car all right.

I put the light in Arlene's face and he took his hand away. The flesh around the hurt eye was swelling. The lid was puffy. He pulled it up part way. The white of his eye was splotched with red, and there was a thin scratch near the pupil. I turned the light off.

"She missed her gouge job," I told him. "Scratch on the cornea, capillaries burst. It'll hurt like hell for a few days, and may be pretty dangerous. We'll drop you off at the hospital in Cheyney to get it taken care of right. Thanks for the help. How'd you know I was hot-boxed?"

"Saw 'em drive up. Figured the pretty Chinese had snapped out of it and would tell 'em. That was nice shooting, man. You're okay, man. In my book."

"I heard that shooting," Karis choked. "God—"

I put my hand on her arm. "It's okay," I said gently. "If you want me to, I'll drive."

"No. I'll be all right. I was scared, Bill. When the guns went off. You don't know!"

The Olds whipped through the night. I stayed close to Karis, my fingers gripping her arm lightly. Little by little I could feel the tension leaving her. Once she glanced over her shoulder at Nathan. Then she smiled at me, gratefully, her teeth pale in the darkness.

I DROPPED THE LAST OF THE PHOTOGRAPHS IN A GARBAGE can in the kitchen of the Fisher home and added a burning match. The smut burned brightly in the middle of the floor for several minutes, became ashes.

Karis came in while the flames were still high and watched the blaze intently. "You burned all of them?" she said, her tongue touching dry lips. Her face was lined with fatigue, and there was a gray smudge of cigarette ash on her cheek.

I nodded. I still kept one of the photographs, one in which Nathan appeared, in my coat pocket, but it would be burned soon, too.

Karis swallowed hard several times. She began to cry without sound, looking down at the floor like a child who has dropped an ice cream cone on the sidewalk.

I guided her to a bright yellow chair and she sat down, sobbing hopelessly in the outrageously cheerful breakfast nook, her face pressed against crossed forearms. She smelled faintly as if she had been cleaning up the bathroom after Nathan.

Between sobs, she said, "He had another headache when I put him to bed. Oh, Bill. What am I going to do? What can I do?"

"You can't be his keeper. If he wants to go to hell so bad, he'll get there in spite of you."

"I've got to do something. *Something!* Bill, you don't understand. I love my brother. I can't bear to see him go on like this."

"Could a psychiatrist help?"

"Yes. I think. I don't know. I brought up the subject once. He raged at me. Said there was nothing wrong with him. Said he was just tired." She laughed convulsively. "Tired."

She looked around the kitchen, seeking some answer to her

despair. "All our life we lived here. Dad died a long time ago. Mother was practically an invalid. Nathan and I, we were each other's family. We played together, all the time. I love my brother. I don't . . . I don't want to see him ruin himself."

"He has the answer," I said. "Kelly. That's what's eating him."

She pressed her hands together, her eyes filled with stark hate. "Kelly Anne? Maybe. Kelley Anne was his weakness. She never cared for him. She spoiled everything she came into contact with. Like a fungus. She blighted his integrity. She must have caused this—this feeling of inadequacy he has. She could do it." Her eyes closed almost painfully, and she leaned her face against her arms again.

I pulled her chair back and picked her up in my arms. She hid her face from me, crying against my neck, her lips open and moist.

"Come on, big girl. You need a good night's rest."

"I can walk."

"You're barefoot. I'll carry you. No charge."

I turned off the kitchen light and carried her to the stairs. She was tall, but didn't weigh much. As I climbed the steps she began to nuzzle my neck, and I was glad to put her down in the bedroom.

She smiled up at me from the bed, passed a hand over her crisp black hair. "I'm all dirty and sweaty. Bill—before you leave, get me a washrag from the bath. And a glass of water and an aspirin, too, please."

I crossed to the bathroom, found a lavender cloth in the linen closet, put it in the wash basin to soak up hot water while I hunted an aspirin. I gathered up cloth and glass and aspirin and started back into the bedroom.

Karis was opening the bottom drawer of her dresser, her back toward the door of the bath. Her dress with the playing card prints was on the bed along with her other things. I retreated into the bath, put the washcloth under the water again to make sure it would be warm enough, tapped my fingers against the basin, ran the venetian blind up and down a couple of times just for the hell of it. I returned to the bedroom. Karis had put on a candy-striped night shirt and was propped up in bed, holding the covers against her stomach.

She took the water and aspirin gratefully, patted at her face with the wash cloth. I sat on the edge of the bed and touched the back of her hand. "See you tomorrow, kid."

She smiled at me and locked her fingers around my neck and kissed me, not playfully.

"Don't," I said, almost incoherently. "Don't. Please."

"You can't leave me now," she said, and she wasn't smiling. "Please, Bill. Stay with me, just for a little while. I'm scared all the time."

I took her hands from my neck, feeling a tremor in them. "Karis, I . . ."

She drew me closer to her, her head against my arm. Her face was pale and very still, her eyes closed. Her breathing was very quick, then slowed gradually and deepened. I put an arm around her shoulders, put my face to hers.

"No," she said softly and contentedly. "You won't leave."

7

IT WAS four o'clock in the morning before I made it to Roxy's. The motel courtyard was parked solid with cars, so I left mine in the drive and went upstairs. Roxy has a small apartment on the second tier of his bar.

He came to the door after a while, wearing passionate pink pajamas. He still had sleep in his eye.

"Glad you made it, Bill. C'min. Be awake in a minute. Have a seat. You look weak in the knees."

In the large living room I sat myself in a low chair across from the studio bed where Roxy had been sleeping. He went to the bath, washed his face and combed his hair, came back looking surprisingly brisk.

"I can put on some coffee . . ."

"Don't think so, Roxy."

"Cigarette?"

I made a face.

"What kept you?"

I shook my head. "We brought him back. That's all that matters."

"Donny phoned in earlier. You had trouble."

"Some. We left a couple of hurt people behind. That Arlene. They had me. He came through in a big way."

Roxy sat on the side of the bed. "He was at the hospital when he phoned. Something about his eye. They were giving him shots. He's earned himself a bonus tonight. So have you."

I let that one ride.

"What kind of shape was Nathan in?"

"Drunk. I think he woke up when Karis was putting him to bed. He had another bad headache."

"You've been over at the Fisher house?"

"Yeah."

"Donny said there were pictures."

"Somebody was taking snapshots from the closet. He had a full view of the bed." I took out the one remaining photo, the one I had saved for Roxy. He got up from the studio bed and took the picture cautiously.

"I burned the rest," I said. "I must have brought home a bushel of pictures like that. I didn't want to take a chance on missing any of Nathan."

"Interesting," Roxy said, looking at the photo. He turned and walked slowly toward an old slant-top desk beside double windows.

I took a cigarette lighter from a low buffet table near the chair and flicked it on. "Roxy."

He looked at me.

"Better burn it," I said. "The wrong people might get hold of it."

A trace of annoyance crept into his eyes before being obliterated by a smile that was a little too warm and friendly to be convincing. "Yes. Certainly." He came toward me almost regretfully and handed over the picture. I touched the flame to it without looking. I had seen too much of Nathan and his poor frantic efforts to reaffirm his looted manhood.

When the flame began to warm my fingers I dropped the charring fragments into an ashtray, stirred the ashes with a fingertip after they had cooled some. Roxy watched me silently.

"You spent a lot of time with her this evening," he said in soft tones.

"Yeah."

"The two of you sorted through those pictures?"

"No. Karis didn't see them. She was upstairs with Nathan."

"Did you make it with her tonight, Bill?"

"What?"

He looked reflectively at his hands. "She's a lovely girl. Tall, graceful. She can be strong as iron. I know. I know how it is with girls like her. I happened to be in the right place at the right time once. With her, I mean. I was surprised.

Afterward, I had a taste in my mouth. Like dark warm blood."

"Roxy!"

He gave me a look of some astonishment. "I'm sorry, Bill. I supposed—well, I supposed you thought she was entirely amateur. I just thought I'd mention the way it is with her. I have nothing against Karis. I hardly know her. It's not her fault."

He turned away and went to the windows, walking stiffly. I put my face in my hands and listened to the beat inside my head. I was tired. I knew I was liable to say almost anything. It was a dangerous feeling.

Roxy said, "A silly thing to be talking about. There are more important matters we need to discuss."

"Like what?"

"I saw Sam Gulliver today."

"Oh."

We looked at each other, Roxy regarding me with faint speculation, wondering if I were still a bargain. He was ready to make up his mind either way.

"I got suspended," I said.

"I know."

"He tell you why?"

Roxy made a movement with his hand. "The Jimmy Herne thing. Sam seemed pretty upset. He seemed to think you're trying to undermine him." I saw the beginning of a doubt in Roxy's eyes that could mean anything.

"Roxy, the other night a body was discovered in the basement of Jimmy Herne's employer, Leland Smithell. The point is, during our investigations we proved Smithell a murderer and thief, and we turned up other information that strongly indicates Jimmy Herne didn't kill Smithell, that he was the victim of a neat frame. I took this evidence to Gulliver, expecting him at least to look into it further. He didn't."

Roxy considered this. "What do you think you can do, Bill?"

"I don't know. I can't make Gulliver reopen the case. But I'll do something."

He turned his head away from me disapprovingly. "I told

you once that it would only bring you trouble if you went out of your way to antagonize him."

He leaned against the slant-top desk. "Besides, if you're right, Bill, you share Gulliver's blame."

"You're not telling me anything."

Roxy smoothed a few errant hairs in his mustache with his little finger. "Gulliver's had three good years in Cheyney," he said reflectively. "There's nothing dishonest about Sam. But he has no refinement of thought or personality. Crude men make mistakes, and their mistakes make them useless. I think the good years are over for Sam Gulliver."

He opened a drawer of the desk and took out a fountain pen and checkbook. He wrote out the check and brought it over to me, offered it with a shy smile.

I took it, looked at it. The check was for five hundred dollars. I felt a weary urge to laugh. I had just found out how much I was worth. I tried to think what five hundred dollars meant to me. I decided it meant nothing, not when it came from Roxy. I gave back the check.

"I'm not for sale, Roxy."

He looked properly puzzled. "I don't know what you mean. It's just a little thank-you note. For helping Nathan tonight."

"I didn't help Nathan," I said. "I'm not qualified. He's a sick baby boy. You better talk to him, Roxy, or he won't be good to anybody."

Roxy folded the check slowly, and put it in the pocket of his pajamas. He seemed oblivious of my warning about Nathan. "I'll keep this. Maybe you'll change your mind."

"No. What I did wasn't for you and wasn't for Nathan. You don't need help and Nathan's beyond it. I was trying to help Karis."

I closed my eyes, remembering her asleep on the bed, sleeping like a child, breathing deeply. She was very lovely, but I knew there was a remoteness in me she could never reach. That no woman would ever reach again.

He nodded understandingly. "She is rather satisfying. Even passionate."

"Stop talking about her." I got to my feet, swayed a little. It would have been easy to fall on my face and stay there for twenty-four hours. "What do you want with Nathan anyway?" I said recklessly. "Are you really interested in his career, or is he just another potentially useful little knicknack like Dr. Einhorn and his wonderful bottle?"

DR. EINHORN WAS TWO HOURS LATE. HIS WAITING ROOM filled slowly with patients, who shuffled in uncertainly with their complaints and ailments and sat tensely in formidable wooden chairs as if listening for a scream.

He came in about ten and distributed apologies. I cornered him before he could go into conference with his office nurse, showed him the badge, requested a few words. He sighed. He was very busy. But he took me to his office and shut the door.

"What can I do for you, Randall?" he said, putting himself in an old swivel chair behind his desk. He wore a brown suit with russet threads and a black string tie. Two deep lines clutched at his large dry mouth like small ice tongs, and there were pads of finely wrinkled skin under his sad eyes. He didn't look well.

"I understand Nathan Fisher is one of your patients," I said.

He nodded. "I've been the family physician for some fifteen years now. Why don't you have a seat?"

I chose a chair near the desk. Dr. Einhorn said, "What is your interest in Nathan?"

"I don't know him very well. But I've seen enough of him to guess he's heading for a crack-up. He goes on periodic drunks. He has violent headaches. He takes up with prostitutes. I wouldn't care one way or another, except for his sister."

He leaned back in the chair, studying me. "I understand, then, this visit isn't an official one."

"No. But don't close up on me, doctor."

He slid open a desk drawer, took out a small box, removed two capsules from the box. He swallowed them, wincing slightly. He replaced the box.

"What is it you want to know? You think I can, or will, tell you what's wrong with Nathan?"

"That's right."

The doctor shrugged. "He gets drunk. He has headaches. He seeks quick, convenient outlets for his sexual energy. Is all this so strange or terrible? He's under a strain. He's launching a political campaign, the outcome of which is vitally important to his career. He lost his wife a year ago. He's the high-strung type. Works furiously for long hours without rest. These things contribute to the behavior of which we speak."

"I could figure that out for myself, doctor. You haven't said a word."

He covered his annoyance with a grin. "Then suppose you tell me what's on your mind, Randall."

"I think maybe his headaches are psychosomatic."

He shrugged again. "I've examined him. So have specialists in St. Louis. You're right about that. We found no organic cause. I suggested psychiatric treatment." Dr. Einhorn chuckled sourly. "He threatened to find another doctor. So I told him I had a drug that might give him relief. The capsules he takes are sugar. They do him as much good as anything will. That, of course, is confidential."

"How did Nathan get along with his wife?"

He pouted slightly, as if it were none of my business, but he answered readily. "He worshiped her. Nathan's an intense young man. He became far too wrapped up in Kelly Anne, so that she dominated his life instead of being just a desirable part of it. I warned him about this. Kelly Anne had a rheumatic heart condition. She was my patient. If she had taken good care of herself she might have lived ten or fifteen years longer. She didn't take good care of herself. She drank too much. She never slept. The consequence was inevitable. Her heart gave out. Nathan was inconsolable. He had tried to get her to slow down, but felt a distinct sense of guilt because he'd failed. I think he'll straighten out before long."

He was silent momentarily. A faint remorseful smile appeared for an instant.

Then he said, "I told you Nathan adored Kelly Anne. Perhaps you know she did not adore him."

"I've heard."

"She was going to divorce Nathan."

"Oh? When?"

"She made up her mind a couple of weeks before she died. They had already been to her lawyer's once. Maybe Nathan's abject love was at the bottom of it. Maybe she was just ready to move on. Maybe it was Karis being a competitor for Nathan's affection."

"What kind of settlement did Kelly Anne want?"

He smiled thinly. His eyes remained constantly sad, as if a part of his mind forever dwelled on his own difficulties. Maybe that was the reason he talked so freely of Nathan.

"I suppose if I don't tell you, you'll find out elsewhere." He glanced at his watch. "I don't know how much she wanted. But I was told it was more than the family could easily afford."

"I thought a sustained exertion on the heart was necessary to cause failure in rheumatic cases," I said. "From what I've heard, Kelly Anne just dropped."

He gave me a smile of approval. "That's true. But Kelly Anne had been drinking with foolish abandon all afternoon. Perhaps she ran up the stairs after something, ran down. This sudden exertion, combined with the effects of the alcohol, finished her. It was a large party, and nobody was keeping track of anybody else. I was there. I got to her right after it happened."

"What did the autopsy show?"

He shook his head. "There was no autopsy. No reason for one. I signed the death certificate." He took a pair of rimless glasses from his shirt pocket and put them on. "I'll have to get to my patients now. I hope I've been able to tell you something about Nathan."

"You've given me some help," I admitted.

He looked over his glasses at me. "I hope you understand," he said softly. "I'm worried about Nathan. I want to help him. He won't let me."

His eyes were glumly intent on his introspected thoughts. I left him.

AT THREE THAT AFTERNOON I MET PHIL NAAR IN A HIGH-
way cafe on the west side of town. He sat in an isolated booth
toward the rear of the place, staring at the table. A cup of
coffee in front of him looked cold and untouched. His raw
white hair was slickly combed and parted in the middle. It had
been a long time since I had seen him with his hair combed.

"Hello, Bill," he said without looking up.

"I didn't know if you'd come," I said uncertainly.

He looked at me then, as I sat across the table from him.
"Gulliver was in his office all morning with two FBI men.
They seemed satisfied that Smithell was Richard Olson. I don't
know what Gulliver told them, what he said about the money.
Or if he mentioned it."

A waitress came and I ordered something to get her out of
the way. Phil continued to stare at the table.

"You know what, Bill?" he said in a quiet, plodding voice.
"I woke up yesterday morning and discovered I didn't like
myself."

"Everybody goes through that."

He looked at me, his eyes hurt and faintly bitter. "No. This
was different. I looked at myself in the mirror. I really saw
me. I told myself, 'You stink,' and didn't feel any pity or remorse. I agreed one hundred per cent with myself that I was
no damn good. I've wasted my whole life trying to kid myself
that I was being useful as a cop. I would have been a failure
at anything else and I would have been a failure as a cop, too,
anywhere but in this town. Maybe you're a failure, Bill. You
failed Jimmy Herne. But you had guts enough to fail honestly.
I would never have dared say a word to Gulliver."

In a way his self-abasement gave him a sort of lonely
strength. I couldn't touch him with pity or anger or sympathy.
I let him alone.

He spoke more rapidly, as if completing vague resolutions.
"I'm through. I'm going to resign. I don't want this town any
more. I don't want the pension checks. I'm going to live with
Jerry. He's the only good thing that's a part of me."

"When are you leaving?"

"Next week, some time. Do you think I'm right, Bill?"

"You're running away from a ghost."

He had anticipated this. "No. Jimmy Herne's not the cause of it. He was just a focal point. When he died I began to think."

He nodded. With one hand he pulled nervously at the metal link band of his wrist watch. "I've made up my mind. What are you going to do, Bill? Go back?"

"I don't know. I haven't even thought about it much. I'm beginning to wonder if I care any more. I've had other things to think about."

There was a zealous gleam in his eye. In the midst of his self-destruction he had sensed the salvation for others. "Why not go back to school, Bill? You're older now, better adjusted. Go back and study law. With your experience as a cop you'd have a head start."

"I'm considering it. Sometimes I think I've had a gutful. But I can't run away."

"If you go back to Gulliver you're still a quitter. You can't do anything now."

I said with a flaring of anger, "Don't try to push me into your mold."

"Sorry," he mumbled. He studied his watch. "Well, I'm due at HQ. I'll be gone in a week . . . I hope I see you before I go, Bill."

"I hope so," I said. We watched each other awkwardly, complete strangers despite years of association.

"What did you want to see me about, Bill? Is there anything I can do to help you—" he began.

"Maybe there will be."

"Tell me."

"I'm working on something now. But I'm not sure what."

"Well," Phil said. "I'd like to help, sure. Sure I'll help. If I can."

8

I HAD no trouble. I went to Roxy's motor court and parked in front of the restaurant. I went inside. There were some people around, in the restaurant. I went up the stairs, to Roxy's office. I unlocked the door, shut it behind me. I took the small brown bottle, sealed with masking tape, from the desk drawer. I put it in my pocket and went downstairs. A few people may have noticed me, but they paid no particular attention.

It was after five o'clock when I reached Highway Patrol headquarters and the office girls were streaming down the broad steps to the street. I walked into the lobby, nodded to a couple of troopers I knew, turned left down a long hallway past Troop F headquarters and the communications center until I came to a door marked *Admittance for Official Business Only* and, in the lower right hand corner of the opaque glass, *Lt. Darryl McHane.*

I went inside. Fading sunlight fell through slanted venetian blinds and striped the floor, tinted the glass doors of the bookcases with sunset colors. My footsteps sounded discreetly on the composition tile. No one seemed to be around. I went through a doorway into the lab.

Lieutenant McHane stood inside with his hands clasped behind his back, scrutinizing a couple of smears on slides beneath petri dishes. There was a towel with many brown stains on the bakelite sink top nearby. McHane wore a full-length apron over his uniform of light blue shirt and dark blue trousers.

"How's the apothecary business?" I said.

He turned without haste and peered at me over rimless

117

glasses. "If it isn't the small-town dick," he murmured. "Long time no see, hayseed."

"You know how it is in my line of work," I said. "Never any time to visit my pals." McHane is a stockily built, meek-looking man with a big nose, morose eyes and thinning hair. He has college degrees in chemistry and philosophy, boasts a vast intricate knowledge of law. This is usually apparent only at trials when he is called upon to testify on behalf of laboratory evidence. He loves to confound smart defense lawyers who fall for his meek act and try to invalidate his lab findings. It's a pleasure to watch him work, although most of the lawyers in the state are on to him by now.

We shook hands solemnly. "Since when are you running your own blood tests?" I asked him.

"Cleve is over at St. Kit's with his bride of nine months and an imminent baby," he said. "I've just been preparing some reagent."

"Have time to do me a favor?"

He wiped his palms on the apron. "Well, you know how bloodstain analysis is. Slow as molasses. Slower. Takes three or four days, if all you've got is dried on a towel like that." He looked unobtrusively at his watch. "What you want done?"

I took the bottle I had stolen from Roxy's office out of my pocket. "I need to know what's in this."

He stretched out his hand. "Let's see." He took the bottle and held it up to the dwindling light of the windows, turned it around several times with his fingers.

"Any idea what it is?"

"Just a hunch. I wouldn't want to influence your decision any."

"Any idea how old it is?"

"About a year."

"Unh-hunh." He took a single-edged razor blade from a cardboard box on the sink and carefully incised the masking tape, unscrewed the lid of the small bottle. He sniffed the contents carefully, several times, inhaling clean air between each appraisal of the liquid. Then he held out the bottle to me.

"What you smell?"

I sniffed a couple of times, frowned. "Whiskey, I think. Pretty faint."

"Can see you're not a drinking man," he said. "Scotch. Good Scotch once, before somebody denatured it with soda pop." He indulged in another long reflective sniff. "Anything else?"

"That's all I could smell. Of course, I don't have your nose."

"True." He stroked the nose fondly with one finger. "There is something else, though. Vague. I can hardly place it."

"Toxic, maybe?"

"To say the least."

"How long would it take you to isolate it?"

"Not long, if it's what I think."

He touched a switch near the door and cold bars of neon flared. I leaned against the refrigerator and watched him. "What's in the ice box, McHane?"

"A pickled stomach, a cocker spaniel's liver and a couple of Coca-Colas," he said. "Help yourself to a Coke. While you're drinking it go into the other room and type out a statement for me. You know what I want on it. Date, time, what you brought in, why. Sign your name."

I did that. I did not mention that I was suspended. By the time I had pecked out with one finger the information he wanted and added my signature he came out of the lab with the bottle.

"I only needed a little of it," he said. "I resealed the bottle."

"What did you find?"

"Scotch and soda pop. Some kind of mixer, I guess. Also a quantity of cyanide. Not a whole lot. Just enough to make this concoction lethal."

I sighed. "How long would it take the person who drank some of it to die?"

He rubbed his nose, pointed to a chair across the room. "After four or five good swallows with some witty conversation interspersed he would about have enough time to walk over to that chair and sit down before it hit him. It would hit him like a tree falling on his head."

"That fast."

"It ain't slow, pal. Not slow at all. Not cyanide. It's a

handy sort of toxicant, too, if you're intent on doing some-body in. Found in silver polish, for example." The glasses slipped a little on his nose and he looked at me over them. "I suppose this will put me in court before long."

"I couldn't say, McHane."

I took the bottle, exchanging it for the information he had requested. He initialed the sheet and folded it, put it away. "Time to stay and talk?"

"I wish I could. I'll buy you a dinner some time next week."

"Fair enough. So long, copper." He turned and trudged back into his laboratory.

Outside the round orange sun was shrouded in haze. Dusk settled swiftly as I took myself and my car home. My feet made lonely sounds on the gravel driveway as I walked toward the apartment house. I used my key to disengage the lock on the door of the basement entrance, and pushed the door inward. The night light inside was out. The door had locked shut behind me before I remembered having seen the janitor put in a new bulb two days ago.

The arm closed around my neck abruptly, crushing the breath from my throat. I was bent backward slightly, so that I couldn't struggle and still keep my feet on the floor. My flailing hands found nothing in the blackness. My coat was slapped aside and I felt the .45 slipped from its holster. Blood thudded in my temples, and there were bright red explosions behind my eyes. I lost interest in trying to fight. I just wanted to breathe. I put both hands to the arm across my throat and tugged.

I felt his breath on the back of my neck, smelled the stale fruity odor of chewing gum. The arm went away from my throat then and I was shoved suddenly. I stumbled against a wall and fell down, held my bruised throat. I whispered a curse. The light came on, and I looked up, at my gun and the man who pointed it at me.

DONNY ARLENE TOOK HIS HAND AWAY FROM THE LIGHT BULB he had tightened in the ceiling socket and grinned.

"Hello, good friend of mine," he said softly.

"What do you want?"

"I came to tell you Roxy wants to see you."

"Why the muscle?"

"Roxy said you might not want to see him. He said this was the best way. I wouldn't hold this gun on you, but Roxy said the badge in your pocket don't mean any more than a bottle top now. You can stand up."

I stood up. My throat was still hurting. Donny waved the gun at the door. "Your car," he said, with a jaunty confident grin. We went outside, and he got into the front seat with me. He had put the .45 in his coat pocket and was holding his stiletto, the blade out. He sat facing me on the seat with the knife hand balanced on his knee, the point of the blade close to my side. He told me to drive slow.

"If I stick you with this," Donny said, "it would make you bleed a lot. Some people get hysterical when they see themselves bleed. I've seen it happen." His lips smacked rhythmically as he chewed gum. He hummed softly. We were going to a picnic, and Donny was bringing the meat.

Roxy didn't smile at me after Donny had conducted me into his office.

"You took something from me, Bill," he said grievously. Somebody had put one over on him, and he was suffering humiliation. "You came into my office and took something from me."

"Took what, Roxy?"

"You know what you took. You took the bottle. I want it back."

"Maybe Dr. Einhorn took it, Roxy."

He shook his head impatiently. "No. I talked to him. He knows better. He says he didn't take it. I believe him. I don't believe you. I know you've got it. Donny, shut up that humming and search him if you haven't done it already."

"No need to bother, Roxy. The bottle's in my coat pocket."

"Get it out."

I took the bottle from my pocket carefully, mindful of Donny and his knife. I tossed the thing to Roxy and he caught it nervously with both hands.

"What was the idea, Bill? What did you want with the

bottle? What made you think you could just take it?"

I didn't answer. To my right Donny folded his knife and put it away. He had one eye on the painting of love among the daisies and the other on me.

"I'm going to call Gulliver," Roxy said. "You just lost any chance you ever had of getting back in good with him. He'll run you right out of town for this." His hand descended to the receiver of the telephone.

"You don't want to call him," I said. "Get your goddam hand off that telephone."

His head jerked up and he stared at me numbly.

"If you do call him, Roxy," I said, "I'll have something to say too. I know about the bottle. Where it came from and what's in it, why it's important. I know all that. Gulliver will listen to me. Even a man like Gulliver has to draw the line somewhere, Roxy. You're way over the line he would have to draw."

Roxy studied me, his face shadowed in the light cast by a standing lamp near the desk. It was the only light in the office. He had control of himself again. He didn't seem worried.

"Why don't you go down to the bar and have a drink, Donny?" Roxy suggested. "Come back in about fifteen minutes."

Donny raised a hand in agreeable salute and left without looking at me again. Roxy sat on the edge of his desk and brushed his small mustache with a finger, as if reassuring himself.

"What do you know, Bill?" he said calmly.

I leaned against the wall near the door, my hands against the smooth cold white leather that partially covered the walls. "The bottle contains a highball with a fatal dose of cyanide. I think Kelly Anne Fisher was drinking it when she died. Somebody put the cyanide in her glass knowing that when she died it would be blamed on her heart. It could have been just about anybody, including you, because Kelly Anne was highly unpopular at the time. I know that Dr. Einhorn suspected or was able to tell she hadn't died of a heart attack and saved some of the drink to prove it."

"And why would Dr. Einhorn give me the bottle?" Roxy said, his voice almost inaudible. He was finding strength somewhere. His eyes were softly confident.

"He made a mistake once," I said. "You were around to mark it down in your book." I walked closer to the desk. His eyes followed me almost dreamily.

"You can't prove where it came from, Bill. You know that. Dr. Einhorn will never talk. You're wasting your time, and mine. You can't prove Kelly Anne died from it. You can't prove somebody put the cyanide in her glass."

"No, I can't prove it. Not yet. I won't stop trying, though."

Roxy laughed, the surprisingly hearty sound beating against the shadowy tension in the office.

"I know, Bill. You'll keep trying. That's why I have to admire you. I should hate you. But you're too much like me, Bill. No. You're more what I wish I could be. You're smart and tough. You're not sure what you want, but you're fighting to prove something to yourself. You'll keep trying to prove that Dr. Einhorn and I are guilty of some crime. But I don't want you to. I don't want you to waste your time. I want you with me."

His voice had become husky, compelling.

"I need you, Bill. I need you with me. Together we can find what we're looking for. Together we'll have the strength to fight anybody." He slid off the desk, stood behind it. "Oh, Bill," he said. His eyes pleaded with me. "What we can do together. We'll go so far nobody can touch us. Men like Gulliver will thank us for allowing them to pick up our discarded cigarette butts. Please, Bill. Don't fight me. Come with me."

"You'll never see the day," I told him.

His eyes widened in dismay. "Bill, listen to me. What do you want? Money, women? You want men to twist like dolls? That's what you want, Bill. You're like me. I know." His face was tight with anxiety, his lips firm with an odd, almost sexual excitement as he tried to measure me within the confined scope of his own desires. "Don't just look at me, Bill!" His voice cracked with an uncertain sob. I said nothing. He leaned forward against his desk, his eyes on my face, demanding. "What do you want, Bill!"

"I want something to believe in," I said. I hadn't been thinking it. I didn't know I was going to say it. But in some way the words represented a final transition, a long delayed completion of manhood. "I can't believe in you, Roxy. You're just a shadow anyway, of bigger men with bigger desires. You don't have any real meaning." I walked up to the desk.

There was a sound that came from Roxy, a tight high little squeal some animal might make in anticipation of death. The middle desk drawer opened. I saw his hand go in and come out. In the chalky yellow light from the lamp beside the desk I saw a revolver in his hand. I kicked out viciously. The lamp fell, the bowl shattering against the desk.

In the darkness I backed cautiously away. There was no shot. I couldn't hear Roxy. I pushed off my shoes and went to my knees, crawled across the rug to the leather-bordered walls.

I waited there.

It was very still.

I waited for what seemed a long time, crouched, breathing shallowly. I waited for him to crack.

After a while Roxy said, "Bill?"

I said nothing.

He repeated, "Bill?" I could hear him move uncertainly then, as if he had shifted his weight. Then something heavy fell against the bottom of the desk drawer.

"I put the gun in the drawer," Roxy said hopefully.

I said nothing.

He picked the gun up again. I heard it scrape against the drawer. He swung the cylinder out, removed the slugs. He dropped them, one by one, into the drawer. He put the gun in, too. He shut the drawer.

I stood up, felt along the wall for the light switch and turned on the overhead light. I put my shoes on.

Roxy looked as if he had just vomited. He leaned against the desk, his face pale. He licked at his lips with a small pink tongue.

"I didn't have anything to do with Kelly Anne," he said.

"Who killed her?"

"I don't know."

"What about Richard Olson?"

His head came up. "Who?" His eyes were puzzled, behind the glaze of despair.

"The man you know as Leland Smithell. He was Richard Olson three years ago when he took a bank in New York for forty thousand dollars and disappeared. Leland Smithell was murdered about ten days ago. He had some of the stolen money in a suitcase in the basement. There could have been anywhere up to fifteen thousand in the suitcase. It was all gone. Whoever killed Smithell knew about the money, took it. Next to the suitcase was a trunk with a dead man in it. Smithell had killed him. Through information about this murdered man we uncovered Smithell's past."

He shook his head. "I . . . don't know anything about that. I didn't even know the man."

"But I think you know about Kelly Anne," I said.

"No. Believe me."

"Does Dr. Einhorn know who killed her?"

Roxy sat down in his chair, his hands folded tightly together. He was through talking to me. He was talking to himself now, silently.

"I'm going to see him," I said. "Don't tip him, Roxy."

He looked up, his eyes blinded by remorse. I don't think he heard me. He was slowly coming unstuck. I could sense the effort he was making to remain whole. His hands trembled.

I went downstairs to the bar. Donny Arlene was drinking Scotch and giving a fast deft line to a slim blonde girl dressed too maturely for her age who sat very straight and didn't look at Arlene, and who seemed to have part of her attention focused on some inward voice.

I tipped him on the shoulder. "Pardon me," I said.

He turned on the bar stool. His smile gleamed. "My friend," he said.

"The gun," I said.

He took it from his coat pocket fondly and gave it to me.

The curly headed blonde had unbent enough to look at us as the exchange was made. Her face was thin and delicately pretty, but immature. She looked from the gun to Arlene, and seemed frightened. As he turned back to the bar the back of his hand trailed along her slim thigh tightly bound in a blue skirt, touched her bare knee. Her fingers tightened nervously on the glass in front of her. She drank. She looked at Arlene, at the dark smooth features. His smile was reassuring. She smiled back, weakly, seemed to lean toward him. Another sacrifice looking for an altar.

DR. EINHORN LIVED IN A LARGE ENGLISH-STYLE FIELDSTONE house cozily wrapped in old ivy in a good section of town. There were lights on all over the house but nobody answered my persistent rings. I tired quickly of leaning on the doorbell and tried the door. It was unlocked. I went inside.

The living room was to my left, a couple of steps down. A staircase to the upper floor was at my right.

"Hello," I said, to the impassive furniture. No one answered. No dog came yapping toward me from within the house.

But there was a sound.

It came from upstairs, indistinctly, so that I listened closely for it to be repeated again, as if I hadn't really heard it at all. I heard the tiny sound of a sob again.

I went upstairs, my feet silent on the carpeted steps. Directly ahead, at the end of a short hall, was a bedroom. I could see the double bed inside. A black doctor's bag was on the bed. All lights were on in this room, too. I went inside. I was following the sound now.

I found him in the bathroom, sitting on the toilet, leaning over the bathtub. He was naked. Clenched in the fingers of his right hand was a double-edged razor blade. There were several scratches on his left wrist. He had tried. His face was clenched, too, as wrinkled as a new baby's, as if he were filled with a sob so gigantic that he couldn't force it out. His lips were parted. He saw nothing. He heard nothing.

On the floor lay a photograph of a middle-aged woman. He had scrawled on it in eyebrow pencil, *Forgive me Martha.* I took the blade from him. His eyes didn't move.

"All right," I said, "all right." I felt afraid. I took him by the shoulder. He didn't respond.

I dropped the blade into a wastebasket beneath the wash bowl. I knew I should hit him to try to bring him out of it. I couldn't make myself do it. I went back into the bedroom. I looked again at his bag on the bed. He could have done it easier. Maybe the draining of blood was to have had some meaning for him. I shook my head.

Someone came up the stairs. A stout woman about fifty years old, hair beauty-parlor gray, body almost shapeless in a light gray suit. She wore a small black hat. The woman in the picture. She looked at me with hard surprise.

"Who are you?" she said, coming into the bedroom. "Where's my husband?"

"Sergeant Randall," I said automatically. "Cheyney police. I came to talk to . . ."

She went by me, into the bathroom, walking with urgent speed. I didn't follow. I could hear her.

She must have looked at him for almost a minute. Then she said, "George." And more sharply, "George!" After a short pause she said, her voice as brittle and fragile as late ice, "Oh my baby, baby, why won't you talk to me, baby? What's wrong?"

She came back into the bedroom. "He's been working too hard. I knew it. I told him. He's been working too hard. What did he try to do it with?"

"A razor blade."

She sat in a chair as if her body was devoid of all energy. "I'll call his brother. He owns a sanitarium not far from here. He'll take care of George."

"Is there anything I can do for you?"

She opened her eyes and breathed deeply. Her eyes showed no sign of approaching hysteria. There was iron in her system, a fine hard core beneath the flabbiness. "I'll be all right. I was a nurse once. I know these things. I'll be okay."

She took the phone from the table beside the chair and placed her call. When she had hung up, she said, "Thank you for being here in time. What did you want to talk to George about?"

"It wasn't important. I guess I'll go now."

"Before you go . . . I mean, I don't want him to just sit in there. If . . ."

I nodded. I went into the bathroom and picked up Dr. Einhorn. He didn't resist me. I carried him into the bedroom. His face still had that look of unspeakable grief. He made a small sound. I put him on the bed.

His wife pulled a chair close to the bed. She sat down near him. She had a Bible in one hand. She took one of his hands in her own. She opened the book, and began to read.

WHEN I GOT HOME I THOUGHT I WAS HUNGRY, SO I FIXED A sandwich and took a bottle of beer from the icebox. I went into the living room to eat, but after two bites I put the sandwich aside. There were too many knots in my stomach. I felt as if I had walked a long way down a far street and turned a corner, only to find myself again on the same long lonely street.

I must have dozed slightly, because the strident sound of the telephone alerted me with a cold drenching of fear. The feeling of dread persisted as I went to the telephone.

"Hello?"

"Bill? Phil Naar." His voice sounded uncertain.

"Yeah?"

"I thought you'd want to know about this. I was over at the Highway Patrol when the call came in." He spoke haltingly. "Some kids found a body in the woods about ten miles west of here. Shot twice."

My mouth was dry. I had to lean against the table. I barely whispered. "Who, Phil?"

"Jimmy Herne's cousin. The Francis girl. Looks like somebody murdered her."

I shut my eyes. I had the precarious sensation of falling, emptily, through black space. "No," I said. "No. No."

"Bill—"

"I . . ."

"I thought you'd want to know."

"Where are you?"

"At the Highway Patrol."

"I want to go there," I said. "I'll come by for you."

"Bill—"

I hung up. I got my gun from the bedroom. I put it on. I remember thinking only one thing. Defiantly. It can't be. It's a mistake. I thought that. It was the only thing that kept me moving. *Somebody's made a mistake.*

9

IT WAS a narrow rutted road three-and-a-half miles from the state highway. On one side were big trees and a split rail fence; on the other was a rolling field. Near a deep ravine through which ran a creek, four cars and an ambulance were parked tightly together. The slope of the ravine was thick with brush and young trees. Headlights from the cars flooded the underbrush with smoky light. There were many men in the road.

We got out. I walked toward the men. Phil trotted behind me. One of the men was Superintendent Sevier, a big man in the Patrol. He looked at me with troubled eyes.

"Where?" I said.

He pointed toward a narrow path through the brush. I went toward it. Nobody said anything to me. There was a spring coiled inside me, ready to whip loose.

The ground was muddy. I slipped a couple of times.

There were a couple of men around her. She was lying on the path, on her side. I saw her in a ring of light cast by two powerful flashlights.

Her blond hair was caked with mud. There was mud on her face, arms and legs. Her clothing was damp. I could smell the clamminess of death about her. Her blouse was ripped open, torn in places. Her breasts were exposed. Under the right breast was a hole, clotted with dark blood. There was another hole just below the first. Dried blood covered her stomach and part of her blouse. Because she had been dead for more than a day and because of the ways death can change a person's face she didn't look too much like herself. Because

130

of that I was able to stand it. I was able to look at her with
some feeling of detachment. She hadn't died easy. My Stella
hadn't died easy. There was a grimace on her lips and her
eyes reflected stilled agony.

I noticed scratches on her hands and legs. Her skirt was
torn, but was still in place. So was her underwear. She held
her brassiere tightly in one hand.

I thought I had some degree of self-possession but somehow
time must have slipped a gear for me and I was unaware of
how long I knelt in the mud and looked at her. I must
have been saying something, because one of the troopers
hauled me up and held me tightly while another, with sad
eyes, slapped the hell out of me.

I shook my head, and blinked.

"All right. Now I'm all right."

The first trooper released me.

I could feel a sudden center of calm inside me, amid a
churning sickness. I looked at the body again and walked up
the path to join the cops.

"I'm sorry, Bill," Sevier said. I knew Phil had been explaining to them. They all wore the same uncomfortable look.

He held his hat in his hands, turning it over and over. He
is a tall man with a receding hairline and a brushy mustache,
and a murky expression. "A couple of kids out hunting found
her about six," he said. "With one thing and another it was
seven-thirty before we got on it. Looks like somebody fell or
was pushed down the path into the ravine. She didn't die right
away, but tried to crawl back up the path. She got around
twenty feet. We found her purse up here. Made the identifi-
cation that way. I'd say about forty-eight hours."

"What about tire tracks?"

"Might have been some. It rained out here late yesterday
afternoon. Hard on tire tracks laid in dust."

"From the condition her clothing was in," he went on, "we
thought she might have been criminally assaulted first. But
her underwear is intact, except for the brassiere. She might
have had trouble breathing as she tried to crawl back and so
tore it off."

"You've got her bag?"

"We went through it. Just a few items. Comb, lipstick, coin purse, a few cards, keys. That was all. Not even a photo."

I leaned against the front fender of one of the cars and put my face in my hands. I stayed that way for a long time, just holding my head gently and not thinking. Most of them went away, to do what they had to do. But Sevier stayed. I felt his hand on my shoulder.

"How well did you know the girl, Bill?"

"I kind of loved her," I said.

"I see." He hesitated, almost as embarrassed. "We hope you'll be able to help us."

"I don't know who killed her," I said. "I don't know who'd want to kill her."

"You'd like to find out."

"Yes."

"What did you get suspended for, Bill?"

"Insubordination covers it as well as anything."

For a moment we listened to the insect noises in the cool summer night, the crackle of sound from the two-way radios in the patrol cars.

"We could use your help, Bill," he said. "Unofficially."

"I don't know what I could do. But I want to help. It's better than sitting around and slowly going crazy."

"Anything you get belongs to us."

"I know that. I'm still a cop."

We shook hands in the darkness.

THERE WAS ONE LIGHT ON IN THE ROOMING HOUSE ON DAVIS Street. The same skinny hairy little man who had let me in last time came from the rear of the house to see who was rattling the screen door. He had added an undershirt and a pair of flopping slippers to the striped shorts. He was eating a dish of ice cream with a tablespoon.

"What do you want?" he said. "Ever'body's asleep. Ever'-body but me. I can't sleep. I got a bowel complaint." He squinted at me through the wire mesh. "I know you," he said. "You was here before. If you want Stella, you're wasting your time. She ain't been here for two, three days."

"Stella won't come home any more," I said.

He continued to look at me. He took another spoonful of ice cream and held the spoon to his mouth long after he had swallowed. A sort of sorrow aged his face. He said a dirty word distinctly, like a soft moan. He put the spoon in the dish and unlatched the screen door. I went inside.

"She—" he began. He scowled, and looked at his feet. "Ah, hell," he said bitterly. He looked at me. "Ah, hell, I don't want no more ice cream." He held the dish as if he didn't quite know what to do with it. "This filthy neighborhood," he moaned. "Always there's somebody who don't come home." A lonely tear slid down his face. "I don't know why I care," he said. "It just means another vacant room. Just another vacant room."

"I want to go upstairs," I said.

He waved his hand and turned his back on me, walked away on skinny curved legs holding his dish of ice cream.

In her room the bed was neatly made, her few dresses precisely hung on the stretched wire. I turned on a small table lamp and shut the door. I went through the drawers of the old dresser carefully, looking for the gold compact which had meant so much to her. It should have been in a shoebox where she had kept odds and ends of jewelry and cosmetics, a few old pictures. I didn't find it there, or anywhere else in the room.

There was a ballpoint pen on the dresser and under it a sheet of paper. I turned the paper over. On it were written two words:

Dear Bill

Beside the dresser was a small cardboard box littered with wadded tissues and a couple of old newspapers. I carried the box to the bed and emptied it. Among the tissues I found a crumpled piece of paper like the one on the dresser. Stella had written more on this sheet before throwing it away. I read the letter she had started to me.

Dear Bill: I know I have not been fair to you but I just could not help myself. I don't think you could ever understand how I felt about Jimmy, because you don't know what it's like to grow up like we did. I'm a little scared now, because before long I think I'm going to find out who killed Mr. Smithell and framed Jimmy. Maybe I should talk to you first, because I might get into trouble. But I've gone this far alone so I might as well stick with it.

Bill, I think I love you. I've been mixed up lately, because of Jimmy. I don't want you to think because of the things I've told you that what we did that night was just another trick for me. Maybe it's too late and I've already made you hate me. Maybe I won't mail this let

I smoothed out the letter as best I could and folded it, put it in my wallet. I went outside and shut the door. In a week the room would hold someone else. It would yield no mementos of the life that had gone before, caught for a while between the dull walls. But I had found just what I needed, a few words hastily written on a piece of paper, to make certain she would go on living for me.

MY LANDLADY, A THIRTY-FIVE-YEAR-OLD DIVORCEE WHO IS blonde, buxom and unapproachable, woke me up by grasping both my ankles and pulling me off the sofa.

"Get up, flatfoot," she said cheerfully. She's usually cheerful except when she's had too much beer; then she tries to eat the bottle. "You're late."

"What for?"

She took my head in her hands and massaged it vigorously. "A man was calling you last night. Every fifteen minutes or so. When he didn't get you he called me. He wants to see you."

"What time—is it?"

"Five minutes to eight."

"Stop beating on my head. I'm awake. Who was it?"

"Somebody named Marko."

I stood up, yawning. She watched me with motherly interest. She has a big bright mouth that could be called generous, two dimples and sexy bruised-looking eyes, and a fine almost-plump body beginning to go to seed. For some reason or other her name is Jennifer.

"What did he want?"

She shrugged. "He wouldn't say. He wanted to see you. Right away. Sounded a little bit excited, in a dreary sort of way."

"Should have left me a note."

"I did. It's still on the door. Didn't you see it?"

"I wasn't seeing anything last night."

"I've got some breakfast downstairs if you want it."

"Don't talk about food. I never want to eat again."

She stared at me. She got up from the sofa and swung her hips a couple of times in the direction of the door. Over her shoulder she said, "Come talk to me when you're feeling better. Or if you get to feeling worse. You can yell at me if it'll make you feel better. It won't matter to me. After what I took from Morris none of you bother me any more. You're all big dumb bastards who don't know anything about women." She winked at me, and banged the door behind her.

I got Roxy's number from my little book and called. He wasn't in his office and he wasn't in his apartment. I put the phone down with a feeling of irritation and went into the bath. I tried to shave. I kept seeing a dead girl in the mirror and my hands were shaky. There was a welling of terrible sorrow in my throat. I had lost my girl. Only I didn't know she was mine. Not till after she had lain in the mud for two days with bullet holes in her stomach. I put my face back together with adhesive tape and went out to find Roxy. He had tried hard to reach me. Maybe he had something worthwhile to tell me.

I tried the office, found the door locked. I could have used my key but I knocked, and waited. I had the feeling that someone was inside. I said, "Roxy."

The door was opened slightly. Nathan Fisher looked out at me, freshly shaven and with his hair combed. His eyes were clear, but slightly puzzled. He stared at me almost apprehensively.

"I was looking for Roxy," I said.

He nodded, as if our thoughts ran the same. "Yes," he said. He was still considering something that obviously didn't make sense to him. "Well, I guess you'd better come in." He didn't move from the doorway.

"Where's Roxy?" I said.

He let me come in then. The blinds in the office were open, and the room was streaked with sunlight in shades of orange and yellow, like a violent abstract painting.

"Roxy's over there," Nathan said unnecessarily. I could see him.

Roxy was lying on the floor beside his desk, on his face. A fuzzy bar of sunlight crawled up his back like a caterpillar. His bright copper-toned hair was matted with dark blood. From where I stood it looked as though he had been shot in the back of the head.

Nathan made a sound like a nervous laugh. He looked helplessly at me and rubbed the back of his neck. "I guess I'm going to be in trouble," he said. "But I didn't shoot him."

"Who did?"

He was becoming more jittery by the second. "I don't know. He was like that when I found—when I came." His eyes went from me to Roxy's body, and back. "I don't know," he said again, plaintively.

"How long have you been here?"

"A couple of minutes. That's all. I just came, and—I just opened the door and walked in, and there he was."

"And there he was," I repeated softly. "The door was unlocked, I suppose?"

Nathan nodded. "Yeah. That's right."

"Touch anything?"

"No. I know better."

I pointed to a chair. "Sit down," I said. I went to Roxy and squatted beside his body, keeping an eye on Nathan. He was concentrating his efforts on lighting a cigarette. When he got it lit he looked around aimlessly for an ashtray, finally dropped the match on the rug after waving it to kill the flame. He gave me a couple of glances, looked morbidly at Roxy's atavistic oil painting.

There had been nothing spectacular about Roxy's death.

He had been shot in the back of the head and that was all. As far as I could tell without moving him the bullet had come out just above the left eyebrow.

The telephone was on the floor beside him, the receiver on the hook. His body was between the phone and the desk and lying across the cord. Roxy had been dead for three hours or more, maybe. It probably would not have been too much trouble to locate the bullet. I didn't want to bother. There were more interesting things to look at.

Roxy's safe, for instance, built into the wall beside one of the white leather panels. The safe stood open.

And on the floor below it, a brown parcel—wrapping paper and ordinary twine. A parcel that might contain money.

I tore it open and the greenbacks cascaded. I carefully counted them. Just short of fifteen thousand dollars.

"My God," Nathan gasped.

Taking out my handkerchief, I opened the middle drawer of Roxy's desk. There was no gun inside. I looked in the other drawers; not there, either.

"What are you going to do?" Nathan said suddenly.

Still carrying the handkerchief, I went to the telephone. "I'm going to call a friend of mine," I said, regretfully.

GULLIVER GAVE ME THE SAME KIND OF LOOK HE MIGHT GIVE to a dead fly in his soup. He wore an unpressed sport shirt and his hair was badly combed. He had taken too much sun lately, and his face and forearms were red. There was a sour grimace on his lips, as if he still tasted bad dreams.

He came into Roxy's office and went to the body and stood very still looking down at it for almost a minute. I couldn't tell what he was thinking. When he was through looking at Roxy he walked around the office once. Then he said to Nathan:

"What time did you find him?"

"I got here about five after eight," Nathan said. "I saw him as soon as I came into the office." Nathan kept trying to twist his fingers off. He was about as rattled as anybody could get.

Gulliver nodded. He looked at me coldly, but said nothing.

To Nathan he said politely, "What did you come to see Roxy about?"

"We were going to discuss some points about my campaign," Nathan said. He wouldn't look at Gulliver. He spoke smoothly, but not as if he was aware of what he said. "Roxy has made some contributions to my campaign fund."

"Did you see anyone entering or leaving the office before you came in?" Gulliver seemed to be speaking by habit, as if he had little interest in knowing the answer. In a mad warped moment apart from the orderly progress of time, I had an image of two blind men earnestly describing a sunset to each other.

"No."

"Was the office door closed?"

"Yes. But not locked."

"What did you do when you found out he was dead?"

Nathan's forehead wrinkled. "I . . . just looked at him for a few seconds. I didn't understand, I guess. Then I heard somebody at the door."

Gulliver lifted an eyebrow in my direction. I nodded. "It was me."

"What did you want here?" Gulliver said. He was starting to come to life again, as he focused on me. He had a look of anticipation I didn't like.

"Roxy wanted to see me. He called me several times last night but I wasn't home."

"What did he want?"

"I don't know. He wasn't able to tell me when I got here."

Gulliver looked reflectively at his stiff wrist. His face was even stiffer. "You can go, Mr. Fisher," he said. "I'd prefer it if you didn't talk about this."

Nathan looked grateful. "No, I won't," he said. He hesitated, then went out the door quickly.

Gulliver followed him, shut the door. He came back and stood in front of me. He looked at me for a while. I looked back, because with Gulliver standing in front of me there wasn't much else to look at. When he smiled at me I was a little too slow to catch on and I couldn't protect myself at all as he hit me. It was a short jab with Gulliver's good right hand and I caught it right over the heart. I could feel each one of his knuckles. Even as I went down with the tearing pain spreading over my chest I knew he hadn't hit me half as hard as he could.

I sat on the floor and held my hands over my heart.

"Ahhh," said Gulliver.

"You . . . God, you dirty . . ."

"You killed Roxy," Gulliver said with a hopeful gleam in his eye.

"Oh . . . give up. Listen, Gulliver. Why don't you give up? You won't find out who killed Roxy. You're too scared of the truth. It would show you up for what you are."

He took a deep breath.

"You were snooping around before I got here, weren't you?"

I looked up at him. I watched him carefully. It wasn't the funniest thing that ever happened to me, getting hit by Gulliver. It wasn't the best laugh I'd ever had. He wasn't going to do it again. If he took one step toward me I was going to shoot his goddam head off.

"Yeah. I saw some things. You'd see 'em too if you wanted to look." I had to stop to cough. "Roxy was probably on the phone when he got it," I said. "Maybe he had just picked it up. When he fell he took the phone with him. Then the killer put the receiver in place so Roxy wouldn't be found so quick. Roxy had a .32 revolver in his middle desk drawer. It's not there now. When you find the slug that killed him, I'll bet it's a .32. Here's another thought for you. Roxy's safe wasn't cracked. So he must have opened it himself, if nobody else knew the combination. There's a lot of money inside. He wasn't killed for that. Roxy collected things, like doctored highballs. He might have had something in the safe that meant trouble for his killer. You just think about those things."

"Get up," Gulliver said. "I'm not going to hit you any more."

"You bet you're not," I said. I got to my feet. "What are you going to book me on, Gulliver?"

He shrugged. His face was composed, but there was a steady look of hate in his eyes. "I'm not booking you," he said. "I don't want to mess with you. I don't want to see you around.

I know what you've been doing. You been effing around the Highway Patrol trying to find out who killed that Francis girl."

"Stop talking about her."

He shook his head in amazement. "The way you go around sticking up for trash like that. You ought to just forget about her. You shouldn't have any trouble finding a better p—"

"I just want to show you something," I said. "I want to show you a letter she was writing me. She knew who was going to kill her." I had the letter out of my wallet. "The same one who killed Smithell . . ."

Gulliver took the letter from me. He looked at it for about five seconds, contemptuously, then ripped it in half. I hit him in the face and felt the shock of it to my shoulder. He went down and lay on his back. Gulliver, with the crippled left hand and the jaw of glass. His eyelids fluttered and there was blood on his mouth. Somebody was breathing like a scared kid. It was me.

He tried to get up and didn't have the strength. He fell backward against the wall, under the painting. He looked at me, his eyes cloudy but still full of hate and humiliation. He wiped at the drip of blood from his smashed lower lip.

Looking at him lying on the floor, too hurt to move his head or speak, or do anything but hate me with his eyes, I felt sick of myself for doing it, for showing him he wasn't as tough as he needed to be.

I picked up the pieces of the letter from the floor and put them in my wallet. It was all I had. He should have known that.

His lips moved, and he talked to me, in a broken voice.

"You're through in this town."

He wasn't telling me anything. I already knew it.

10

I DON'T know why I went back exactly. But I couldn't stand being alone with myself and anything was better, even being close to the memory of her lying twisted in the mud with holes in her belly.

They had taken her away by then, of course. On the slope of the ravine birds hopped through the underbrush, and a squirrel posed on the path, watching me. The sun was hot on my face, and there was a smell of damp vegetation drying.

I didn't have much money, but I was going to spend it all on a funeral for Stella. I had talked to Kenwick that morning. He had cleaned her up, washed her hair. He would comb her hair and put on a clean dress, the best of the dresses from her room. I chose a plain coffin in dark red wood with a little silver trim, for the girl with the lonely uneven life, for what we might have had. There would be flowers. Those who lived at the rooming house were making up a collection. Phil Naar had sent a basket.

I walked down to the creek and sat on a large brown rock close to the sluggish water. I thought of Stella, the Stella I knew, the right Stella. I couldn't remember her clearly, this Stella I knew, remember all the good things that made it easy for me to love her because I believed in her. There was a cloudiness in my mind that made me think of her in many beds, giving wantonly to many men. I tried to think of Leland Smithell with his hands on her. It was impossible. There was no picture.

Reason came slowly. It was impossible for Stella to have done that, with him or with many others, because it would have changed her just as surely as it had changed other girls from the rotting neighborhoods who lived too freely too young. My personal knowledge of her was too strong to let me believe in the other Stella she had told me about.

I didn't try to think any more. It was all right now. I sat on the old rock in the sun and felt nothing, except a pleasant warmth in my stomach. The knots had loosened. I had the feeling that she was close to me, somewhere. I guess I was a little crazy. Not enough to worry about. Everybody is a little crazy sometimes.

Something else was coming, and I let the meaning gather slowly in my mind, a piece at a time. I wasn't in a hurry any more. I would stay here until I knew.

It must be that she had lied to me that night in Smithell's basement, even knowing what it would cost both of us. But she had lied anyway. I believed that. She lied so I wouldn't find out why she was really there.

She couldn't trust me. She couldn't depend on anybody but herself, and because of that, she was shot.

A picture in my mind. Of Stella standing in the road above, her back turned, eyes shut in terror. Flashes of gunfire. Stella down, fingers spread over her stomach and side, rolling down the path while birds soared in fright and clouds covered the sun.

Feeling nothing, I could see her get to her feet, fall, face blank with pain, get up and fall again and try to crawl and drag herself a few feet and then stop with blood warm in her mouth. Lying on her back and fighting it hard but without strength to go on. Realizing then she had to find some way to tell me.

What had she done then, in the last desperate seconds? She hadn't been able to find a way to tell me who.

I went back, to the night in Smithell's basement. The memory of it was blurred. Too much shock crowded into minutes had burned deep into my mind, but the burn had scarred over. Images stuck erratically to the edges of consciousness, like cut-out pictures pasted in a child's scrapbook. Stella, falling in the spray of light from my flashlight. The dead thing in the trunk. Stella's fingernails digging at my cheek. I raised a hand to touch the faint scar that still remained. Why had she done that?

I stood up. The warmth was gone from my stomach, and I could feel the knots tightening again. There was a dry taste of remorse in my mouth.

I knew why Stella had gone there that night. Maybe it also explained why she was killed. But it didn't explain who.

Or did it?

I started up the path. I went slowly, as Stella must have gone. Near where she had stopped, unable to go on, I stopped.

Her blouse had been ripped open. It was muddy. There was mud on her bare stomach and exposed breasts. One nipple scraped raw from contact with the ground. In her hands she held her brassiere, twisted tightly, as if in one last expression of agony.

As I said, maybe I was a little crazy, and it didn't mean anything. Maybe she had taken it off so she could breathe easier. But it wouldn't have been easy for her to remove it. She might not have tried unless it was meant as a final message.

I repeated it to myself. Over and over again.

"Bra—bra. Brassiere—"

If it was a message, then I had something.

I WPNT TO MY CAR AND DROVE BACK TO CHEYNEY. ON THE main street, which is cleverly known as Main Street, I parked in front of the store I wanted. I went inside. There was no one in the place but a salesman. The store smelled vaguely of silver polish. It also smelled of money. It was the best of five jewelry stores in town.

The clerk, whose name was Mr. Simms, was impressed by the badge, so that he got overly serious and exaggerated his every movement trying to be casual.

I explained what I wanted: a girl had come into the store recently, with a compact. She had wanted to trace the compact back to its original owner. I described the girl, and the compact, as best I could.

"Sure. I remember the girl. Blonde. She brought in one of our compacts. One of the specials. We have them made to order. She said she found the compact, wanted to return it to the owner. I looked up the description and sketch of the compact in our files and found who it belonged to." He scratched his nose, looked at me earnestly.

"How about looking it up for me?"

"Don't need to. I still remember. It was made especially for Mr. Nathan Fisher." He seemed disappointed that I showed no reaction. "I can find the address for you if—"

"Thank you," I said. "I know where he lives."

I went outside. It was close to five-thirty, and there was a hint of dusk along the street. Above me soft tubed letters of green flared on one at a time, then all glowed proudly at once. BRASSIER'S, the sign said.

Epitaph in neon.

"GULLIVER," I REPEATED. "LET ME TALK TO HIM."

"He's not here," the desk officer said. "Hasn't been in all afternoon."

"Any idea where he is?"

"No. Fishing or something. I don't know."

I thought for a minute, tapping my fingernails against the receiver of the telephone. "Phil Naar around?"

"He was, a minute ago—*Hey, Phil!*—hold on just a second, Bill."

He came to the phone quickly enough. "What?"

"Where can I get hold of Gulliver, Phil?"

I could imagine a thin smile on his face. "What for? You want more trouble than you already got?"

"No. There won't be any more trouble. For me or for anybody."

"What's wrong?"

"Nothing's wrong. I just need Gulliver."

"I don't know where he is, Bill."

"Look, Phil. Do something for me. Now's the time for that help you promised. Find Gulliver for me. It's important."

He didn't answer right away. Then he said, "All right. If

it's important. I'll try to find him. What should I tell him?"

"You don't need to tell him anything. Just take him to the Fisher place. I'll be there."

"I don't—"

I sighed and hung up and left my apartment. I went downstairs to my car, and drove to the Fisher house, taking my time. It was a fine summer evening. Children and dogs played along the quiet streets, in late sunlight.

Nathan Fisher came to the door to let me in. He looked old, worn. His shirt was unbuttoned at the throat and he wore slippers on his bare feet. He carried a full ashtray in one hand, a fresh cigarette in the other. His face was uncared for and his eyes were tired, not pleasantly tired, but as if he had been hanging by his thumbs for half an hour.

"Hello," he said. "Why don't you come in?"

I went in.

"I guess you came to find out more about me and Roxy," he said. "Let's go into the living room. I don't suppose you know any more about it than you did this morning."

Nathan apparently had been working. There was a briefcase beside the sofa and papers were scattered over the coffee table. Nathan put the ashtray on the coffee table and switched on a table lamp.

"I'd offer you a drink," he said, with a faraway laugh, "but Karis—"

"Where is your sister?" I said.

"Karis? Oh, upstairs, I think. Washing out some things." He went to the hall and called up the stairs, "Karis!"

"What?"

"Nothing. I just wanted to know where you were."

Her voice came nearer. "Who is it?"

"Bill," I said.

"Oh." I heard her walking down the steps. She and Nathan came into the living room. She was wearing Bermuda shorts and a casual buttonless overshirt. She smiled at me.

"Bill."

I hadn't seen her since the night we had brought Nathan back. I looked at her, thinking about the fine slim lines of her body, but completely without pleasure.

"Hello," I said.

"Nathan told me about Roxy. Bill, do you have any idea—?"

"I've got some ideas," I said. "That's why I'm here."

"Oh," she said. She sat on the arm of an easy chair. Nathan took a seat across the room. I didn't sit down.

"Do you think you know who killed him?" Nathan asked me.

"Yes," I know. "I know who killed Roxy and Stella Francis and nice Mr. Smithell down the street. I know who killed them all, and Jimmy Herne too, indirectly. I'm just not sure why." I looked carefully at him. "I'm not sure why, but I think I can make some accurate guesses."

He looked back at me, tired eyes interested, but lips tight at the corners.

"Think," I said. "Did you ever give a compact to anyone? A small compact from Brassier's?"

"Yes. Why?"

"Who did you give it to?"

"It was a Christmas gift to Karis."

In the taut silence, my voice sounded angry and thin.

"I know why you had to shoot Stella," I told Karis. "When she found your compact in Smithell's bathroom and traced it back to you, you had to get rid of her. Maybe Stella didn't know how important the compact was. But she was convinced Jimmy had been framed and she was ready to follow any lead. I think you got scared because that compact linked you too intimately with Smithell. It wasn't hard for you to kill her. You already had some practice. Stella thought she might get into some kind of trouble, but not that kind."

"What are you saying?" Nathan demanded. "What are you—?"

I turned to him, still keeping an eye on Karis. But she wasn't going anywhere. "I'm saying your sister is a killer. I'm sorry, Nathan. I have to take her in."

"You—you're crazy," Nathan said emotionally, "You goddam—"

"Why don't you ask her?" I said.

"Karis," Nathan said. "We don't have to listen to him. I'll throw him out of here. This is the most—*Karis!*"

He was out of the chair before I could stop him.

"Karis, don't just *sit* there! Tell him—do you want him to think—" He kneeled beside her. She didn't look at him. Her hands were folded between her knees. Her eyes looked at a happier time.

Nathan's face was falling apart. Then a crazy sort of hope that he could make some reason of disaster put it together again. "Karis, listen baby, please talk to me, I know this is a shock, but he's crazy, he doesn't know what he's saying, I know you didn't do that, Karis . . . Karis, *Karis!* Look at me, G-god damn you, oh no, no . . ."

He slid to the rug, put his face down between his outstretched arms on the seat of the armchair. He sobbed loudly. Karis closed her eyes, an expression of unspeakable pain on her face.

"What . . . did you . . . do to me?" he sobbed faintly.

She looked at him then. "No," she said anxiously. "I didn't mean to hurt you."

"I don't have to guess why you killed Smithell," I said. I knew I was only talking for myself, but I wanted to put it all together and say it, just once.

"You knew about the money in the basement. You probably found out sleeping with him. Maybe he talked in his sleep or maybe he just felt like bragging once. Nathan had a long hard campaign coming up, and he needed money, lots of it. So one night you took your problem to Smithell, asked him for a sizeable contribution to Nathan's campaign. Naturally he told you to go to hell. The next thing, you probably tried a little polite blackmail. I can imagine how he would have reacted to that. He was a pretty hard character, a killer himself."

"So he got rough with you. Maybe there was a struggle in the living room. You picked up the candy dish and hit him with it. Only hard enough to stun him. He fell against that end table, upsetting the lamp, and it clipped you on the ankle. If he was still conscious he tried to grab you, so you hit him again. Maybe several times, because your ankle hurt and you were mad. But one of the times was too many and his skull caved in.

"The first thing you thought about was the money, so you took his key and cleaned out the suitcase in the basement, not knowing what was in the trunk. Once you returned upstairs you had a problem. You could always call the police, claim Smithell made advances, and maybe never serve a day for killing him. Nobody would find out about the money either. But it was risky. And the newspaper stories wouldn't help Nathan any. On the other hand, all of Smithell's friends knew about Jimmy Herne's record. So it was easier to steal the watch and jewelry and pocket money and set Jimmy up for the frame. Even if the frame collapsed it would at least be diverting for a few days. But it worked better than you could have hoped."

She was crying now. "I shouldn't . . . I shouldn't . . ."

"No," I said. "You shouldn't have brought Jimmy into it. As long as it was between Smithell and you it wasn't too important. But when you framed Jimmy you started changing other people's lives. Jimmy wasn't much but he deserved more of a break than he got from this town.

"You gave the money to Roxy for safekeeping, and to spend on the campaign as needed. I suppose you knew Roxy fairly well through Nathan. You did it with him a couple of times, too. You just can't resist anything in pants—including your brother. You might have told Roxy the money consisted of anonymous donations from wealthy friends—money they didn't want to show up on any of your bank statements. Roxy was passionately interested in Nathan's career and wouldn't ask any questions.

"But Roxy got upset when I told him about Smithell's past and the money stolen from his basement. He put two and two together gradually and tried to get in touch with me. Roxy wasn't going to have anything to do with murder. When he couldn't get me he called you. When you couldn't explain adequately where that money came from, Roxy opened his safe, tried to get you to take the money. You wouldn't touch it. Too hot now. So Roxy decided to call Gulliver. If you knew Roxy at all you knew about the gun in his drawer. He liked to point it at people. So you took it out and shot him in the back of the head. You must know how to use a gun because I've seen you carrying a target pistol."

Nathan's sobs still sounded spasmodically. Karis said nothing.

"One more thing to clear up," I said, my mouth dry. "Kelly Anne. Nathan's wife." I saw Nathan lift his head. Karis saw it, too.

"From what I've heard Nathan was crazy about her and she didn't give a damn for him," I said. "You didn't like her, probably hated her. When she got ready for a big divorce and wanted more money than Nathan could afford to pay her, you decided Kelly Anne had to go. A messy divorce would have played hell with Nathan's career and smeared the family good name. You are pathologically fond of your brother. So you slipped a little cyanide into Kelly Anne's highball and that would have been that except for Dr. Einhorn, who was suspicious enough to save some of the drink and analyze it. Since Roxy owned Dr. Einhorn he found out about Kelly Anne too. He was saving the information to use at a profitable time; say, when Nathan became governor."

"But what can you prove, Bill? Not a single thing," Karis said, almost idly. Her big brother was on his knees nearby, looking up at her blindly, his mouth slack.

"I only need to hang one killing on you to send you to the gashouse," I said. "It'll take some work but it can be done. You killed too many not to have made mistakes. We'll find somebody who saw you with Stella just before she was shot. We'll find traces of her in your car. We'll find the guns that killed Stella and Roxy, if you haven't had sense or time enough to ditch them in the river. Sooner or later we'll nail you to the wall, Karis. It's just a matter of time. And I'm going to be with you every step of the way until you die."

I didn't know she could move so fast. She came off the chair, her hand picking up the full ashtray from the coffee table, and I caught just a glimpse of it before she flung it at my face. The heavy glass just missed but ashes stung my eyes, clogged my nostrils and filtered into my mouth. I gasped and choked and rubbed my burning eyes, giving her the chance to follow the ashtray with a shoulder block, ramming her elbow into my stomach, and I fell backward over a chair. While I was on the floor she snatched my gun and eluded my blind grasp.

"Get up," she said.

I blinked my eyes and saw her through a misty film. She stood about twenty feet away, holding the gun on me steadily. I saw Nathan crawl toward her, get to his feet.

"Karis!"

"Don't come near me, Nathan. Please, darling, don't come near me."

He stood close to her. "Karis, God . . . why?"

Her lips pulled away from her teeth in a grimace. "That bitch," she said softly. "That dirty blonde bitch. Why did you have to marry her, Nathan? I tried to tell you she was no good. I tried to explain, but oh Christ you were so in love, you couldn't listen to me, and find out how cold and vicious she was. She never was any good for you."

"Don't," he begged. "Don't—please don't talk about her."

"You wasted yourself, Nathan, you wasted yourself on her. I had to kill her. I had to. We were happy. We didn't need anybody else. I love you. Didn't I always take care of you, Nathan? Didn't I?"

She smiled vaguely at her brother, her eyes sad. Gentle blue eyes, so soft and deep a man could lose himself forever in them. Her voice was as muted and clear as a beautiful memory.

I stopped coughing. I watched them. I watched this thing happen. I never thought to make a move toward her while she was occupied with him.

"Karis, put down that thing," he said, with a horrified face. "You're a killer. You're insane! Go with Bill." He grabbed at her.

She struck him in the face with the barrel of the gun.

He didn't fall. Blood welled from a rip in one cheek. She had to hit him again and this time he went down to the rug. Blood was streaming from his torn face and trickling down his chin. Karis looked at him. He was shaking all over. He grasped his sister's bare legs and pressed his face against her knees, smearing them with his blood. He made meaningless sounds. She raised my gun again. When the barrel bit into his skull near the hairline his hands jerked away from her and he turned a little before collapsing. She had hit him all three times with a pleasantly vacant expression as if she were stroking a cat.

I jumped for her then but it was foolish because she had the gun on me before I could take two steps and the barrel bucked up and I felt the slug slam, felt impaled on a lance. I stopped dead and swayed stupidly. The bullet had creased somewhere near my right collarbone.

Her lips twitched a little and she looked slightly surprised that I lived. She aimed the gun again and I twisted desperately toward her . . .

But the shot never came.

The front door had banged open. Gulliver stood in the hall looking at us.

We all looked at each other while every clock in the world stopped ticking.

Then Karis swiveled and the spell was broken. Gulliver went for the gun on his hip. He's not slow with that small gun of his but Karis shot him two times before he could bring the .32 into play. He went down on the rug, face down, his arm outstretched and the revolver clenched tight in his fist. I saw his arm move and thought he might get her after all but one of the bullets had taken off the bridge of his nose and there was so much blood in his eyes he couldn't see to shoot anybody.

I took three clumsy waddling steps in her direction. She hadn't turned around yet and I thought maybe I had a chance to get to her. Anyway, I had some crazy idea about not just standing around waiting for the next bullet.

When she did turn she held the gun almost at arm's length, which is the only reason I'm still living. I reached out and grabbed the barrel and twisted the gun so she couldn't pull the trigger and fell against her and yanked the revolver from her, all this with my good arm. She went over backward and I pinned her down but let the gun go. I only had one good hand and I tried to get her by the throat but my fingers had turned to wood and my strength was going. She picked up the gun by the barrel and started hitting me in the face with the butt.

It was as if I had fallen a long way into a pit and was lying on my back watching it happen to somebody else. I didn't feel the blows too much but I knew my face was being ruined because she had hit me at least five times after the first one knocked me into the pit. I just kept holding onto her after there was no reason to and finally she pushed me out of the way and got up and that's when everything became impossibly blurred and distant, though I didn't lose consciousness completely.

In a few seconds or a few minutes somebody found me and tried to help me. I couldn't see. Blood in my eyes. I couldn't hear either. Words were a jumble of sound. Finally things made sense, with the first sharp thrust of the pain. It felt as if my whole face were hanging from my eyebrows, in scraps. I set my teeth together. Strangely, I still had all of them.

I got one eye open some. I saw Phil Naar through a filmy red haze. He supported me in a sitting position. I saw the handkerchief he had been using on my face. It was a mess. There were pieces of me on it.

"I called the hospital. They'll be here. Hang on, boy. Gulliver's bad, too. Shot up bad."

I thought I was going to die then. The wound. I just had that feeling. I was scared. "Did you get her?" I said, without moving my lips.

There were tears in his eyes. "Bill. I couldn't do it. She came running out of the house and I could have cut her down half a dozen times. But I couldn't do it. I couldn't shoot her. She took the squad car. I called the Highway Patrol. She won't go anywhere."

I felt the pinwheels starting. "I'll be okay," I told him. "You better get a towel and try to help Gulliver. I wouldn't want him to die now."

I went away from the room then, as gently and as easily as if I were wrapped in folds of black velvet.

11

THE HOSPITAL corridor was long and clean and quiet in the morning sunlight. I finished signing for twelve days' room rent and assorted services and walked slowly up the stairs to the second floor. Phil Naar waited there for me. He looked strange to me in the blue uniform with the Chief of Police arm patch. But he wore the uniform as if he had been in it all his life, instead of a week. There was a quiet sort of pride in his eyes.

"Morning, Bill."

"Hello, Phil."

"All checked out and everything?"

I nodded.

He hesitated, and looked at the tips of his polished black shoes. "I don't suppose you've changed your mind any?"

"No. I guess not, Phil."

He shrugged. "Okay. I know how you feel."

"Come on," I said. "I want to get out of here."

We walked down the hall and into one of the rooms. Gulliver was sitting up in the bed. He was bare to the waist, and great strips of tape covered his chest. His doctor had inserted a drainage tube at his side just below the armpit. Gulliver's face was pale, what we could see of it. There was more tape and gauze across the middle of his face. He breathed through his mouth.

"Ten minutes," the nurse said, "and don't excite him." She went out and shut the door.

We looked at each other uncomfortably for a few seconds. Gulliver breathed noisily through his mouth. Then he said, "Guess your face is going to heal up all right, Bill."

"Yeah. Changed around a little. A couple of more scars. They won't show much."

"How's the shoulder?"

"Stiff. It'll loosen up."

"Good," Gulliver said, nodding soberly. "That's good." He looked at Phil, curiously. Gulliver had never worn his uniform unless he had had to. "How are things with you, Chief?"

Phil seemed a little uneasy. "Running smoothly. Nothing much happening."

Gulliver nodded again. "Well," he said, "It's pretty dull around here. This is about the first time I've been able to sit up. So the drain will work." He tried to laugh. "Wish I had a good cigar. Doctor says it would be too hard on the lung I've got left."

He scratched at his jaw. "Nobody ever told me what happened to the girl," he said, looking first at Phil and then at me.

"She tried to drive through a roadblock about twenty miles west of here," I said. "The car flipped over and slid upside down into some gas pumps in front of a filling station. Everything blew sky high. She burned to death."

"What about the politician? Her brother?"

"He had a nervous collapse. He's getting psychiatric treatment somewhere. He'll be as good as new one of these days."

Gulliver smiled sourly. "Better than us, Bill. Better than us." He frowned. "I'm not bitching. I got off lucky, I guess." He looked at me. "You know, Bill, I thought he did it. I really thought that Herne kid did it."

"Yeah."

He picked at the sheet that covered his legs, watching the movements of his fingers. "I was wrong about the Francis girl. What I mean is, she had more backbone than I thought. Just like the kid. Tough."

"I'd tell her," I said, "if I knew where to get in touch with her."

The nurse came back into the room. "I've got a pain," Gulliver said promptly to her.

"Where?"

He took her hand and guided it beneath the sheets. "Right

here, honey," he said, grinning at her shocked expression. He
winked at me.

I went outside. Phil came out a few seconds later. We shook
hands.

"So long, Phil," I said.

"Look," he said. "Bill, do you blame me?"

"No. It's what you wanted. I know you'll do a good job."

"Thanks." He smiled with dignity and brushed at something
on the front of his coat. He looked at me. There was a
little wave in his white hair. He looked very neat and efficient.
In a way it was funny. But everybody has a dream somewhere.

"What are you going to do, Bill?"

"I don't know. No plans. I might get out of these parts for
a while. Change of scene."

I handed him my shield.

"Keep it," he said. "Something to remember us by."

I put the shield in my pocket and went downstairs, not hurry-
ing as much as I wanted to. It seemed a lot easier to walk
slowly through the hall and pause on the steps just outside the
doors of the hospital. And look across the trees of the park
to the buildings of town. I watched an airplane, silver in the
clear air across the river, rise slowly and powerfully from a
long smudged feather of factory smoke.

It was a hell of a town. And it had been a hell of a life.

There was a vague ache in my chest.

And what about all the Jimmy Hernes in it?

No one in his right mind would . . .

I put a hand gently to my healing face, as if it would tear
if I touched it too hard. I felt a grin starting and couldn't
stop it. I called myself all kinds of names and the grin got
bigger. I put my hand in my coat pocket and my fingers
closed around the badge there. The names stopped pounding
into my head.

I turned around and pushed through the glass doors of the
hospital and went back down the hall. I walked fast. I broke
into a run and took the steps three at a time and stopped to
catch my breath when I reached the second floor. He was still
waiting there, standing in the middle of the hall. When he saw
me he walked toward me slowly, and I waited for him.

"I missed my bus," I said.

He looked at me without much expression. Bright sunlight from a window splashed across the blue and gold front of his uniform like gossamer armor.

"The kids like Jimmy, in trouble. Maybe I'll be able to help them."

He shook his head and smiled.

"I hoped you'd think of that," he said.

We walked down the stairs together.

THE END